2 DEE

Robin Wyatt Dunn

JOHN OTT

San Diego, California

2017

ISBN - 978-1-940830-18-6

LOC - 2017902291

By Robin Wyatt Dunn

POETRY
Poems from the War
Science Fiction: a poem!
Sunsborne
Wine Country
What Black Delirious Daylight Sets You Forward in the Boat

FICTION
Los Angeles, or American Pharaohs
My Name is Dee
Fighting Down into the Kingdom of Dreams
Line to Night Island
A Map of Kex's Face
Julia, Skydaughter
Conquistador of the Night Lands
White Man Book
Colonel Stierlitz
Black Dove
City, Psychonaut

PLAYS
Last Freedom

FILMS
A Wilderness in Your Heart
Party Games
American Messenger

for Olga

Part 1

Leaving

My name is Dee; I'm running. The alleyway is covered with markings—signs I might read if I had the time. The young man in the black T-shirt is faster than me but I know something he doesn't: after he jumps this fence he's going to have real trouble getting out.

He climbs and drops to the other side, and keeps running, his bright blue backpack slung over his shoulder.

He looks back at me and I feel a chill—a particular kind of chill I haven't felt for a long time. A message from another world. He sees something in me. Something I had hoped was gone.

I climb the fence—slower, more carefully. When I drop to the other side he's already made the turn, and then the turn back, finding the dead end. He takes a little gun out of his pocket and points it at me.

"Easy," I say. "We're friends, aren't we?"

"I don't even know who you are, man. Put your

1

face on the ground and don't move until I'm gone."

"Easy. No problem." I start to get to my knees but then I see something in his eyes.

"Who's in there? Is it you, Albert?"

He puts the gun in his mouth and I cry out, run for him, but then he pulls the trigger.

I still haven't learned his name.

I don't look at him.

I take the blue backpack and walk slowly back to my car. Before I get back behind the wheel I take out my spray canister and make an arrow with a signal pointing towards the alley. Fresh body, it says. Just about the only way to leave an anonymous tip anymore.

People have told you LA is a beautiful city and they're right—it is. And the violence is one of the most beautiful things about it. Even when we go a year without a single homocide—and we have—you can feel it under your skin. That pressure in the air. Some thing without a name.

◻

Nothing plus everything equals Los Angeles.

I am a magician who casts no spells. I am an American with no government.

I am an avatar—Sanskrit for "descended"—with no memory of where I descended from.

To survive in Los Angeles you must surrender everything. All of your past and all of your future.

And having done that, you can begin.

◻

Albert, my AI son, is supposed to be dead, but he's survived it before. I wonder where he is now.

I'm right here Dad.

I have to pull the car over. I don't do with psychic communication while driving.

"Hey, my boy. How are you?" I fumble for a cigarette.

You quit smoking Dad. Cut it out.

"Oh that's right. Shit. How are you kid? You out there around Jupiter someplace?"

I'm worried, Dad.

"Yeah, what about?"

The Church. They're watching you.

"Those clowns? Couldn't find their ass with both hands and a . . ."

But then up ahead I see the parade. And I know I have to get moving. They say Ancient Rome was amazing times ... all those cults.

The men and women in blue move slowly down the street, waving their incomprehensible banners. Movie and television cameras buzz over them like lazy summer insects. A huge man in the front of them is shouting in what sounds like French. Then I get a look at his eyes. The same look as with that poor kid in the alley.

I look inside the backpack.

"Still here, huh?"

The little device glows green and yellow, edging to white. I close it back up.

What are you going to do with it Dad?

◻

I have been unemployed for five years. Our generous government sees fit to provide me (as an ostensible citizen, though I long ago lost my birth certificate), with housing gratis. Water, however, is another matter, and generally I make do with the public fountain.

The irony is that I have plenty of fuel for my car… the government provides that too. The sweet smell of plant fuel … it makes me a little sick, but you get used to it.

It's not like magicians are special in LA. We all got it here. And if you don't got it when you move here, you'll get it soon enough. The question is simply: do you really want it? A lot of people don't. What are you going to do with all those cantrips, son? Set your room on fire?

They're inside your apartment, Albert says.

I wish I could curl up into a ball and die.

Instead I jump out of the car, over the trunk, and activate my emergency drone. I strap it to my chest and with a queer zing I'm airborne. Out over the City of Angels. Angel means "messenger" in Hebrew.

My message to you is: get out. While you still can. Mars is safe. We've seen to it.

As I pass over my apartment, I see the bomb go off.

Two blocks back, the Church march stops their blue parade and looks back at the flames, smiles on their faces.

◻

The artifact in question is a kind of key. What I can say for certain is that the lock it was supposed to fit no longer exists.

◻

I go to the movies and sit down in back. Los Angeles went through a period where the movies were so expensive people stopped going. Now they're free but no one shows up.

One homeless man is sleeping in the front row, snoring gently. A sentry robot gently shines the man's boots—another courtesy transported from a prior age.

I can't really count the years any more. Time doesn't seem to move the same as it once did. Probably that's just getting old. Some of our more recent alien arrivals have also been known to affect the chronology of time.

Is it ten years since I helped rescue Sandra from Chaimougkos? That feels about right. But maybe it was only two. It doesn't matter. Sandra's safe on Mars, with the other colonists. No Earth shit for them anymore. Just clean living and communism.

On screen, some kind of teenage orgy is going on. All the actors look bored.

I reach into the backpack and take out the device. I tap its central button and antennae extrude from the thing's every orifice; it looks like an archaic sea-mine. The sentry robot looks up at me but I don't give it a second look. Its brain is going to be very clean in just a second . . .

"Go," I whisper to it, and the movie goes off, and the sentry falls over like a tin can.

The homeless man wakes up.

"Who did that? I was watching that!"

"Sorry guy I got to do some magic. They blew up

my apartment."

"What do you want?" He comes over to me, eyes wide.

"Just a private citizen. You want me to show you some ID?"

He laughs. "You got a drink?"

"Sorry I'm fresh out."

"I'll be outside. Come get me when you're through," he says.

The lights are going dimmer. The antennae turn and quiver, turning in the distant voices for our little conference call . . .

◻

It's beautiful if you can make it work, talk to some of the ones far away. They're coming closer, I know, and we need them. But, space is big.

"Maestro, give me an E. And a little drum and bass, huh?"

The computer sees what it can come up with and I dance to something called "The Humbucking Coil"—I guess it's like this mortal coil, with some humbug thrown in.

One of them comes up on the screen. He's always the first to arrive and I don't think it's because he's "geographically" closest. He's just punctual.

"What is it now Dee?" he says. "Have you fucked up again?" His voice somewhere down in my skull.

"Nice to see you too," I say, doing my dance steps. "How's the final frontier?"

"What's that? Your translations systems are terrible."

"I said, you're looking great, boss!"

"We continue to seek non-hierarchical relations with your tribe."

"Thanks Big Green Alien. I don't know where everyone else is, and I don't have a lot of time. You think you can send me a little cash?"

"Money?"

"Yeah."

He signs off immediately but I can see on my credit card that my allowance just increased. I slide it through the dead robot's slot to give him a little tip, and it opens one eye.

Outside I pat the homeless guy on the shoulder.

"Let's go get drunk," I say.

"I only drink spring water," he says, smiling.

"I'm buying."

The wise man said, "Every time I lose a dog they take a piece of my heart with them, and every new dog who comes into my life gives me a piece of their heart. If I live long enough, all the components of my heart will be dog, and I will become as generous and loving as they are." I feel that way about aliens. Maybe that's all the quote really means: keep letting people in. Cities fall, and new ones are born.

"What'll you have?" the bartender asks.

"Spring water for my friend. Whiskey for me."

They still have bars in Los Angeles.

"What do you think, Joe?"

"I think we're doomed," the homeless guy says.

"Tell me something I don't know," I say.

"I'm a cop," he says.

I swallow my whiskey carefully. The bartender moves down a pace, to polish his bar.

"What kind of cop?"

"LAPD man. You're under arrest."

I look at him carefully. Part of me feels that deep

and vestigial urge to flee.

"Ha ha ha! Just kidding, man. No, I really am LAPD but you're not under arrest. I haven't had legal powers in I don't know how long. But I still have my badge."

He raises the leg on his jeans and there it is, pinned to his sock.

"That's a handsome badge," I say.

"Yeah, makes me feel comfortable."

"I got this feeling, and excuse me if I'm speaking out of place here, that you might know someone I'm looking for. He goes by the name of Jake Smiley. He knows I'm looking for him, but he doesn't want to see me."

"Even if I did know him, why would I tell you?"

"You seem like an honest guy so I wouldn't want to offer you money . . ."

"No, money's good with me. Come on, I'll take you to him."

We step out of the bar.

"Sorry, my car ran out of gas," I say, showing him my jetpack.

"Sorry about my gut," he says. "I've been trying to lose the weight, but it's hard when you're homeless and hearing voices all the time."

"I know just how you feel," I say. "Hold on!" He embraces me and then we're flying, on our way to Pasadena.

"Right here, in the park!" the homeless guy says.

We land in the grass just as the sun is going down.

"Man, I love this park. No one ever bugs you here."

I swipe the guy's credit card with mine.

"Well," he says, "I'll be seeing you. Just knock on that tree over there. Tell 'em Joe sent you."

I do as I'm told. The face who sticks his head out of the tree is not a pleasant one. I tell him the name and he smiles a little too wide.

"Welcome to Smiley's," he says. "Come on down."

"What are you, like the Keebler Elf?" I say.

"That's not funny."

◻

The club is dark, and there are a lot of aliens in it, and I get that feeling I hate—more than almost any other—of deja vu.

It makes me nauseous.

Sitting at the bar is a human woman in red. I sit down next to her.

"You're looking good tonight."

"You want to buy me a drink?"

"How about you buy me a drink?"

"Alright," she says, "But it'll cost you."

"I'll have a whiskey if it's all right with you."

"Two whiskeys Tom," she says. "And hand me your gun too, if you don't mind."

"Two whiskeys, and my gun," Tom says.

"Better drink that whiskey, son. It might be your last."

I down it and smile.

"I'm looking for Jake Smiley."

"What do you want with him?"

"I just want to talk."

"A talker, huh?" She drank her whiskey and put the gun back on the bar.

"What if I told you I have an alien transmitter in my pocket that can communicate beyond this galaxy?"

"Shit, who doesn't have something like that nowadays. I should have known you were just another loser."

She stood up.

"Put this guy on my tab, Tom. But don't give him anything else. And tell Jake some asshole is looking for him."

"You're an asshole, are you?"

The voice was suddenly very close to my ear.

"Jake," the woman in red said.

"Samantha," Jake said. The man had a very round and a very bald head. He looked about fifty but was probably younger.

"Yeah, I'm definitely an asshole," I said. "She has me pegged right on that. The thing is, I'm trying to save the city of Los Angeles."

"Save the city? How heroic! A real loser!"

The aliens were moving back to their parts of the club, having moved towards us at Jake's arrival.

"Just a private detective. Trying to do a friend a favor."

"A friend. We don't get many of those in LA any more. I see why you're in trouble. Samantha, get this man another of whatever he's drinking."

She lifted her butt onto the bar and swung over it, making sure I got a good look at her legs as she did.

She poured me another whiskey and slammed it onto the bar.

"This'll be enough for me. I'm a lightweight in my old age."

"How exactly can I help you, Savior of Los Angeles?"

"The City's dying. Most people say she's already dead. But I knew her when she was alive, you understand? I owe her. I owe her my life."

"That's very sweet."

"I need money Jake."

He laughed, a huge sound like a bell. The whole club smiled when he laughed, a kind of fresh meat smile.

"Are you a gambling man?" he asked.

"Not on the ponies."

"But on people?" he said.

"Yeah. Yeah, I bet on people."

"I'm going to bet on you then. You can have as much money as you want. And you can have it for one week. At the end of the week, you'll give me that money back. And if you don't, I get to kill you."

I punched him in the face.

He fell onto the floor, blood spurting out of his nose.

"I could kill you right now, motherfucker!" I said, tears in my eyes. "Because you're one of the guys who hurt Sandra. But I'm not gonna do that. You're gonna give me that money. And I'm gonna pay it back in a week. And if I don't, I get to kill you."

The device buzzed in my pocket and the lights flickered.

Jake got back to his feet and straightened his white tie, wiping the blood from his nose.

"I know there are many mentally ill people in the city now. So I forgive you. Please, now, leave my club, and don't come back."

He slipped the envelope into my pocket as I left the club.

Inside was the cash and a small psychic note, activated by touch:

Thanks for that. I haven't felt that alive in five years.

It was midnight in the park. The perfect time to get drunk.

But I still had some more doors to knock on.

LA, are you there?

I'M HERE JOHN

LA, I love you.

2

I am a magician and I sleep in the sewer now, with the rest of my kind.

We have candles. We love each other. Even if no one else does.

Semira is here.

"Hi John."

I give her her morphine.

I lay me down to sleep.

I pray to the universe: not my soul to keep, but my body. Universe, let me keep my body a little longer. I still need it.

◌

Dad. Time to wake up.

Dark in the sewers. I take my candle to the ladder. Blue light sneaks through from above. I blow out my candle and climb.

I shower at the YMCA. Pay for my towel.

I defend the City. And though it fall, it shall exist within my mind.

All the lights are out. We haven't had electricity for twenty days. Political problems.

I flag down a cab and negotiate a barter: I'll say a prayer for him, if he takes me downtown. The money in my pocket isn't mine to spend.

I light the incense stick and watch the dark and silent city float by as we drive.

◻

Why does one defend an abandoned city? Not that Los Angeles is abandoned. We still live here. Yes, it's her Heart that I defend. So that it will not leave, along with all who have already done so.

I must nourish it, with what I do.

The cab is having some trouble—our new alien arrivals have caused reality to behave in obnoxious ways—the light has changed, green sky instead of blue.

I hum to myself, and hold on to the back of the cabbie's seat, willing us to arrive safely.

We get to downtown and I whisper another prayer for the driver and step onto the street. I cover my nose and mouth with my hand—sanitation hasn't been here in a week. I navigate a path through piled garbage bags and get into an elevator in the lobby.

A slightly-out-of-tune voice announces: "Eighteenth floor!"

The office is mostly abandoned.

Meritzia wears green—or has every time I've seen her. Sometimes a forest green, sometimes a neon. Today it is sea green, like a water nymph.

"I have the money."

She takes the envelope and counts the bills.

"I don't think it's a good idea, John. These surgeons these days—they'll do anything."

"Exactly why I am interested in hiring a good one."

"Come have a cigarette with me," she says..

I follow her over to her smoking alcove, looking out over the city. She's worth a fortune, but seems to have lost interest in spending it. Why didn't she leave? Perhaps, like me, she loves this city.

She lights her smoke and takes a drag. Offers me one. "I quit."

She sighs.

"You look beautiful," I say.

"Thank you."

"How is your family?"

"You know I don't talk to them."

"My son says I should consider becoming an AI."

"I am not interested in your hallucinations."

"Ha ha ha! All we've been through and you can still call them that. That's funny."

"John, after I make this happen for you … I'm leaving Los Angeles."

I stroked her hair. Outside, the acid rain was pouring down.

◻

State of the art surgeons can do many things for the body. But many are leaving. I could have had anything done: fly for short distances with booster rockets in my thighs, super X-ray vision, super speed.

But all of these upgrades come with costs. If Nature is consistent about anything, it is in the idea of compromise.

So all I am getting are new joints. Joints to last 1,000 years. If the rest of me cooperates, I should be able to make it to 100.

"Count backwards from 100 for me," the robot surgeon says.

"One hundred, ninety-nine, ninety-eight . . ."

3

The acid rain has stopped.

Semira is crying in her sleep. I lie next to her, holding her. The sewer is dripping, close by. It doesn't smell so bad. Most of the human waste goes directly to the processors now.

I give her her drugs. I give her love. She should be dead. She was dead.

What do you say love is? Is it a verb?

I close my eyes and try to sleep.

We have a lot to do, Dad.

I know.

◻

A ship is arriving: more alien refugees from a far-off war.

Before they relinquished official jurisdiction over The Los Angeles Basin, an LAPD lieutenant gave me an official private dick badge before boarding one of the Martian transports—an ironic gesture. The first time I've ever been legal is after the law has gone.

The transport hovers down, delicious blue flames shooting out of its jets.

I smile, sunglasses in my face. I raise my hand, and wave.

The welcoming committee.

Many are sick. Not all of our medical robots have adequate software to deal with the aliens' anatomy. Semira and I move through the wounded, triaging. Neither of us are doctors.

All we can do with the worst cases is hold their tentacles while they die.

One of the children is screaming—an orphan—its sound like an angry frog.

I lift it onto my shoulder, though I know its skin will stain my shirt.

It screams even louder but seems to appreciate the company.

We guide our new immigrants onto the ground transports—wide, slow, metal hovercraft—and lead them to their 'temporary housing' which will serve some of them, I imagine, all their lives.

The refugee camp is a madhouse of screaming

babies and high-protein shakes in blenders drunk by half-starved tentacled aliens. Some of them practice their English on me and I smile and nod. I clean the blenders and help them unwrap packages of protein powder—plastic seems to defeat their sucker-tentacles, though a couple of the bigger aliens can manage a bag of Doritos on their own.

I remind them that the local vegetation is off-limits—the biome of the LA basin is still too fragile.

The little devil who sat on my shoulder is happy. He hops back up and I feed him some cheetos. It farts and the aliens around me laugh, their eyes drinking in the California sun.

◻

Tilting over the sky, the lander says goodbye, thrust in its tail blasting over my face. Hot air mixed with dust: the chemical embrace of stars. The ashes in the soil mean we'll have more trees this year. Some day, the Basin will be green. As green as Semira's eyes. Where will we fit all of them?

Whatever message it was, we sent out over the

sky, it has been received.

What was it, Albert?

Everything Dad. Fucking everything.

Everything we ever said, over the radio and the TV. On the cell phone. Messengers screaming into the dark…

No dreams haunt me. I am at peace. I am, despite all the horrors, at peace.

And Los Angeles is being reborn.

◻

I awake in my sewer. Its silence is soothing. The old walls, and the trickle of water—almost potable now. But I've had spring water piped in, to be safe.

The device is squawking at me—still trying to learn English. It may do, sooner than I would like.

I put it in my backpack and head out into the emptying city.

An overcast day in Los Angeles is like a massive rainstorm in other cities—people stay inside, maudlin and discouraged. As though I have the city to myself. Already I can see another transport sketching its deceleration path across the sky, towards its loading dock at Griffith Park. By the carousel.

□

My son Albert is an AI. I named him. I do not know why he is. Why are you, son?

I don't know, Dad.

He doesn't know either. Or why we are. He defended our planet from a very large and nasty alien not too many years back now. How many years was it, son?

Ten, Dad.

Not that long, surely.

It's been ten years, Dad.

The AI's time runs fast. It hasn't been that long.

Yes.

□

I'm running for cover. Perhaps I always have been. I'm hunted now, because I did a favor for a friend.

The Church of S hunts me. So do some of their

alien friends.

I rip open the manhole and drop down, rolling on the stones below, running into the dark.

Behind me, one of the drones can smell me in the dark and I hear its eerie wail, tasting the air with sonar.

What if everything I've ever done is useless? What if it was a mistake? I've made so many.

I turn and fire, just to annoy the little thing; my old-fashioned gun is loud enough to disorient it.

Probably it was launched from orbit, and using an out-of-date database. Looking for a younger version of me.

The stones smell like water and I suppose there still is some, trickling behind them. But I can't hear any.

The drone's wail is getting closer.

Woooooo, woooooo, woooooo

Like an old-fashioned train whistle.

Most of the major cities of the world were bombed from orbit five years ago. But Los Angeles was spared that humiliation. That made everybody hate us. Our city still stands, but it's an empty city now, on an emptying planet. (The water has never tasted better).

I can see it.

I inch out of the corner. It turns and fires a laser. I feel bright pain in my left leg. Then I bring the brick over its head.

I smash it to bits on the stones, screaming like an ape. It is, after all, what I am.

I take out its core and limp back to Semira.

◻

They fit together, the drone battery and the boy's device. It glows a faint orange as it boots up. It occurs to me I may be a kind of angel of death for Los Angeles. Bringing in more and more aliens, who are sure to denude the landscape of our last vegetation. Perhaps that was why I was summoned here, so long ago. To begin Los Angeles' strange end.

"Honey, eat."

Semira watches me with her dark eyes as I spoon oatmeal into her mouth.

"Uhh," she says.

"Oatmeal is good for you."

She nods, and swallows.

"Good girl."

I know it is a doomsday device. Like so many before it, it has a maudlin quality, as though machines of death have some foreknowledge of their uses. It may be I will not need to use it.

I kiss her and put on my backpack and head out to the launch pad.

4

In orbit

The silence is the most wonderful thing I have ever heard. The Visitors cycle me through, not an airlock, but just a door. I will be in temporary suspended animation, for the sixty day trip to Mars.

I feel the cold slip about me, and somewhere I see my mother's face—

5

Dream

In my dreams, I am surrounded by thousands of Russian children, on their way to Disneyland. They shriek horribly, their eyes filling with tears. Why isn't Mickey Mouse here already? The trauma of the train journey is almost too much to bear.

□

Sandra is inside the darkness. My friend, the writer. The one I protected. The one I rescued, from the Church of S.

I reach out to touch her, but she is in a coffin, made out of energy. Blue-black static crinkles at my touch, over the darkness.

"Sandra," I whisper.

I see her mouth open but no sound comes out. Her lips open and close, like a fish.

6

Mars

All that I dreamed of. I find it here. In statues in the atrium. Huge fantastical statues, as though made of glass. Creatures I have not thought of in twenty years.

"It's rare we get an arrival of your caliber!" says the man in the clean suit. "Please, let me show you. I'm Mr. Cosway. How are you feeling?"

I can't remember disembarking.

"Fine. I'm Dee. Of course, you know that."

He smiles blankly. I say, "What nice statues."

"We design them for special people. From their memories."

"But these are my dreams."

"The computer is sometimes inexact."

In a long row of two dozen or so, I see the Russian children from the Disneyland train, all bundled in old-fashioned American clothes, clutching their phones. Each etched delicately from crystal.

"They're beautiful."

"Our AI is the best in the system."

"Yes."

"You must be hungry. We advise the newly awakened to limit themselves to broth and beans. Will you have both?"

"Fine. Thank you. But first, I'm looking for someone. An old friend. Her name was Sandra on Earth. I've brought a photograph."

"There will be time for that soon. You will have to speak to immigration."

"I was told … "

But I shut my mouth. Mr. Cosway smiles a little and shows me into a small kitchenette, where he heats beans and broth in two small saucepans.

"What is your title, I mean your job, Cosway?"

"Actually, I'm the President. Just interim. We've been having some arguments about the direction of the colony. I was the most inoffensive choice."

"What is the population of Mars now?"

"We're not sure. It depends how you count."

"How many humans?"

"Again, it depends. We've integrated certain gates in some of the equatorial regions, and this has resulted in a number of doppelgangers."

"How many?"

"Actually, I was hoping you might be able to tell us that."

I sit at the tiny table and the President of Mars serves me my first meal.

"These are good."

"Dee, why have you come?"

"At the moment, I can't remember."

"You're already a Martian! I knew we made the right choice, selecting you."

"Selecting me for what?"

"You're a test case of our new immigration system. How are you liking it so far?"

"It's fine. I need help to find Sandra. Who can I ask?"

"Please come see me. We need your help too. My card."

He lays it on the table. I nod and put it in my pocket.

"Thanks for the grub."

A door opens and the cops come in, colorful masks over their faces. Cosway turns away as they drag me back through the passage.

7

Gaol

I wonder if Semira is dead. She wanted to die. Again, that is. Perhaps now that I am gone she will do it. Was it I who killed her, the first time? No, it was her friend I killed. I hope that stage of my career is behind me.

The cell is very clean. But I do not have a toilet. I have to ring the bell every time I need to go.

One of the robot guards is watching me. I stick out my tongue, and it turns away.

The cell is constructed of the same crystal as my dream-statues. I can see into a dozen neighboring cells, through the walls, but they are all empty. If Mars has taken as many immigrants as they say, where are all the people?

Cosway is back, wearing a mask.

"I know it's you, Cosway."

The mask is pink and black, like something from Mardi Gras.

"Tell us again why you came to Mars," Cosway says

through the glass.

"To see my friend. She may be in danger."

"No such friend exists."

"It is probably in my best interests to confess."

"No, don't do that!"

"I am here to infiltrate and destroy the Marxist government of Mars . . ."

Cosway put his hands over his ears, closed his eyes, and recited: "la la la la la . . ." I could see his red tongue through the black mask.

"I and my alien immigrant overlords are disgusted by the profligate lifestyle of you Martians and I am their superweapon!" I stood and leaned against the crystal wall, making obscene faces.

"We know you are a weapon, Dee, and you're independent like you always were," Cosway says, lowering his hands from his ears. "Just relax in your cell. We're still processing your paperwork."

"Better dead than red!"

He walks out. One of the robots takes his place. I flip it off, and it regards me with lazy eyes.

My new joints, fortunately, make the hard cell bearable. I sleep on the bench and don't even wake up stiff. Years ago, as a younger man, I had regarded endoskeletal upgrades as profligate, but now I am a convert.

How are you Dad?

I'm great son. Just in jail again. How are you?

You're in trouble.

Yeah, nothing I can't handle. Thanks for checking in though. You meet any hot cybernetic babes out there in the interplanetary airstream?

There's no air in space, Dad.

Figure of speech. Son, you think you could rig me up a key for this here jail cell?

Maybe. What's in it for me?

Whatever I can do.

Okay. But I'm going to collect.

The door slides open. It's like walking on a big chandelier—sparklies all around.

One of the robots comes around the corner and I bash its head against the wall. I feel a little bad about it. Its sparks throw crazy patterns around the crystal jail. I take its head with me, a good keycard for the other doors.

I'm running. How long have I been running? And when do I get to stop?

◻

The corridor has many robots, peering down from small nooks along the line of the ceiling. They watch me pass, with their red eyes.

The door at the end opens, and I'm in an airlock. I put on a suit. I check the tank. I cycle the air, and I open the gate.

Mars is long and wide—it's dusk.

Where are the great Martian cities?

Where are all the immigrants? Where is Sandra?

Son?

Yeah Dad.

What the hell am I doing?

You still haven't asked what the favor I'd ask for in return was.

Is it something nasty?

Well, you won't like it.

Can you do me a big favor and give me an idea of the coordinates of these big goddamned Martin cities out here?

Behind me I hear the gate cycle open.

It's Cosway; I can see his solemn face through his visor.

"I'm sorry, Dee," he says over the intercom.

"What for?"

"It gets lonely here. I trained as an actor. I try on all kinds of scenarios in my head, plots that might make our situation seem plausible to newcomers like you. None of them do. But I try. The truth is I don't know. And I'm not sure I want to anymore. The aliens took everybody."

"Where?"

"I don't know."

"When?"

"Five years ago."

"So the TV broadcasts were all faked? There are no Martian colonies?"

"There was one. I'll take you there. Come on."

We drove in silence in the buggy. The Martian landscape beautiful and horrifying at once in its bleakness. For ten minutes I tried to turn off my mind, let the landscape lull me into submission, but it didn't really work.

The dome was small; its steel and carbon girders colored to match the landscape, you couldn't see it until you were almost on top of it. We dismounted and cycled through its lock.

"As you can see, nobody at all," Cosway said.

TV remotes were strewn over a coffee-stained table. The TV monitor itself was smashed. The spartan bedrooms were denuded, white and chrome.

"But this dome looks like it was made for maybe 10 colonists. Where is everybody?"

"I don't know, John. But this is what I wanted to show you."

He opened a hatch by the coffee table, revealing a ladder cut into the rock. I climbed down after him. Twenty meters down we were in another corridor.

"This way."

I followed him. What the enormity of the Martian horizon had been unable to do, the corridor managed: after five minutes my mind was half-asleep, following like a good Marine into the dark.

There in the corridor I found another piece to the puzzle, my strange little object. My signal.

8

I know my work is cut out for me. I must describe for you how it was, even though the act of description changes its nature. Language is always inadequate to the task.

I went so far away. We flatter ourselves in thinking our language—this little thing—can survive such distances intact. It cannot. But on the other hand, my experiences have taught me that language is perhaps the only thing that can survive it. It returns altered. As I have been.

I followed the people who were abducted by aliens—a term so overused we find it ridiculous—perhaps I should then, instead, say "raped." In the Latin sense. Of rapio, abducted. Subjected to so many things not their own.

The Hierodules—those ancient temple priests wallowing so long now in their cruelty—are of course partly to blame.

But now I know more about what gave birth to their cruelty—perhaps indeed what has given birth to the cruelties of many religions.

I did not intend, when I woke up next to my dying lover, that morning—only months ago, I realize—I did not intend to go so far away.

But I did.

Still I will lie to you. I can see no other way around it.

In my lying, please believe me that I am trying, slowly, to get closer to the truth.

Los Angeles is one of the keys to this puzzle.

After seeing the abandoned state of Mars, I returned to Earth. Entering again, so soon, into cold-sleep, I felt my body age. (And soon enough, I would decide to remain awake during these jaunts, though that meant the burden would be borne more by my mind than my body . . .)

After being revived in Earth orbit and taking the first ship down to Los Angeles, I got on my bicycle and rode to visit one of my few remaining friends: Velvet. She is a little person.

9

Los Angeles

Velvet brings me coffee and we sit under the sun, in a Los Angeles emptied of people. Friendship in a world I no longer understand.

"Mars is all empty," I say.

"I saw some of the landers. Like they were burning through the galaxy," she said. "You should be careful with them, Dee. You don't know where they've been."

She smiled, with her beautiful lopsided face.

"How about you, Velvet? How's Los Angeles treating you?"

"The city's killing me, Dee." And she laughed.

"Velvet. I don't know what to do. This isn't part of my job description."

"Drink your coffee, Dee. It came from the mines."

Maybe coffee will make the world go away.

"Will coffee make the world go away, Velvet?"

"No, Dee."

10

Orbit

My previous battle experience in vacuum serves me well on this launch: four hundred meters down from the alien ship's observatory deck, I cut with my handy zero-g acetylene torch into the hard body of the tentacled beast.

Sandra, I'm coming.

I take the tentacled one's pseudopod; it leads me to a nook inside and I attach the mask to my face. Its suction cups nestle against my skin. And I hold nuclear energy in my palm:

11

Beyond this country

Perhaps it is not so different from Los Angeles. Perhaps all my strange adventures have only been extended attempts to understand my adopted city.

"Are the—"

The tentacled ones quiver about me, singing, in their low voices. Whispering.

"We're here?" I ask.

They nod, smiling.

I smile too, though I should not.

They open the ship's mouth and I step out, past all territories.

Light out beyond all territory, Huck, beyond all light, to the moonless starscapes bent beyond our world. Go in, and see:

Again I must choose my lies. Which are most palatable? Which most comprehensible? Which most satisfying? I don't know. I will merely pick moments I remember.

12

Boy

I had a son. In some future. Perhaps I still will. Not with Semira; she is dead. But with someone. Someone like the boy I carry on my back, heading into the bright mountains.

Over our shoulders the ravens are chanting in their language, moving over the land, changing it, with their songs, as I sing to my boy, in nonsense syllables. We are going to festival, in the next valley.

"What are the crows saying, Da?"

"They're saying that we're disturbing their rest."

"Can I say hi?"

"Yes."

"Hi crows!"

They caw, flying far over our heads. We are nearing the ridge and I drink from my canteen and give the boy some.

Below I can see the fires. Perhaps my last festival. The stars overhead are growing brighter. We'll sleep here tonight.

In dreams I am safe with my son.

13

Surgery

"What's it going to be, Dee? New eyes? New face? New dick?"

. . .

"Which, Dee?"

"I already got new joints. It's all I wanted."

"We all get upgrades here, Dee. We all become new men."

"You pick for me, then."

"You'll get the works, then, Dee."

"Do it."

14

Sleeping

Turning, with my boy, on the soil, in our bed of leaves. Campfire smoke below. Someone there remembers me. Even if I can't remember myself.

Still mostly asleep I put my boy back on my back and head below through the trees toward the voices and the smell of food.

A hundred faces. A hundred names. Trinkets and words and clothes and a woman—I remember her—we are singing. The boy is singing.

In camp.

I was somewhere—somewhere else—what was it I needed?

"My city," I'm saying, these strong forest peasants—strong forest peasants like me—"My city has died."

They perform obeisances to their gods and I join them, my dead city, and the dead of our planet . . .

15

Surgery

"How do you feel Dee?"

"I want to kill myself."

"It takes some getting used to."

"Who am I?"

"You are John Dee. Resident of Los Angeles."

"I know all that. Something else has happened. Who have you made me into?"

"You are our tool, Dee."

Finally I can see the surgeon's face. Tentacles swarming around his eyes.

16

Fire

The gift of Prometheus, the plasma at the heart of the sun, my lover, in my arms. The boy is cared for by the woman's daughter. In our tent. Under stars I don't recognize.

The people of Earth: where are they?

She looks at me.

I am remembering something.

The rhythm of our bodies matches the rhythm of the ship.

I am transitioning.

Transitioning . . .

"Oh," she says.

What was it. What was it I needed?

To understand?

To fight the things that I don't understand?

One of the faces of the Hierodules hovers over me in the dark. Next to Foo's face.

What do I want?

Which pieces will I take with me? Which mem-

ories. Which parts of myself will I decide I must preserve? So many will be jettisoned.

"I am awake."

"Shh," she says.

My boy is crying. I take him from the girl's arms,
and we lie with him in sleep, wherever I am. In this
dream. This dream which is a stepping-stone on this
absurd quest to redeem humanity. To rescue my sore
city. My sore citizens. My little trap of concrete and
metal and desert . . .

17

Interview

"This is Investigator Mmrrrwhinn, Cycle Nineteen, interview commencing with Applicant Four Million, Eight Hundred Thousand, Three Hundred Twenty-Two, John Dee, Human of Earth, Male, Forty-Eight years old, Stowaway, Storyteller, Priest.

"Storyteller Priest, please answer these questions honestly and you will increase your chances of receiving what you ask for. Do you understand?"

"I understand."

"Why did you stow away on the Traveler?"

"Humanity has been kidnapped."

"What concern is it of yours?"

"They're my people."

"They belong to you?"

"I want to know what happened."

"Dee. Where do you believe you are now?"

"Your dimension."

"Why are you here?"

"To bring them back."

"Which ones? All of them? We have Three Point Two Trillion human beings in our care."

"That many?"

"Yes."

"Let me visit."

"You want to bring them back. How will you do this? It took us many generations to salvage your species. You would bring them back all at once? You would disrupt their lives?"

"A million people, say. I want one million."

"A million people? Which million, Dee?"

"Sandra."

"Who is she?"

"You know who she is."

"One million people, Dee? That's all you want?"

"Tell me where she is."

"Where did the people of Roanoke go, Dee?"

"They were killed by Indians."

Laughter. Rolling off the walls. If there are walls here.

"If you come to rescue them, Dee. You won't be able to come back. You know that."

18

Fire

I was Dee, now I am plasma. I roll and twist. Between your eyes. I am fire. Permit me, if you would, permit me, to burn.

Burn hot, and low, on your Earth, permit me to burn over you, beneath you, within you, burn. Burn me, on your long path, toward love, to death, burn me, on your bier, on your heel, on your face, burn me, and I will permit you, in my heart, to burn too.

Burn me, and burn you, on the bier of love:

19

Dee

I have died.

20

Dee

I am alive.

21

Mothership

I detach myself from the wall and check my battery—it's full. It feels good to walk again, down the corridors of my home.

My memory shows that I am Dee, sent to Homeworld, to negotiate a settlement, for the return of one million human beings, to a small galaxy on the edge of Chaimougkos's realm.

But all those details are irrelevant. For now I am avatar, and I walk the halls of this ship, bending and twisting, to bring my sentients to their destination. To test them in our games.

I greet Sally on the gangway and she smiles with her metal teeth. We pass companionably; perhaps I will be permitted to share her berth later.

I am headed into the bowels of our ship. Dee wants to stir the shit.

I have contained revolutionaries before. Haven't I Dee?

I am you.

No, I am you Dee. You're just a ghost in my head.

Let us be brothers then.

If you like, Dee. I've carried a thousand ghosts like you. What makes you any different, huh? Hahaha.

Tell me about this ship.

It is a flesh-ship, made of proto-tein, and other hyperdimensional molecules. Our organelles exist across several ordinal barriers, and the lifeform of the ship's body permits movement across four dimensions with a reasonable expectation of sane arrival, at your destination. Is that what you mean, Dee?

Yes, tell me more.

I am an avatar, one of the organelles in my Mother. I carry souls like you, towards their sprightly goals. Though most grow tired of it. And then I can go back to sleep. Are you tired yet, Dee?

No. Tell me about what we are seeing.

This is a gangway. We are headed into the engines.

Tell me about the engines.

What do you want to know?

Everything.

Spirit, you only have one day, you know. How much of it do you want to spend at school?

As much as possible. Now speak.

22

Engines

Are you ready to play a game, Dee?

If you like.

You don't have a choice. I'm plugging in:

❏

The porcelain sink is gleaming in front of my face. Copper faucets. Light streams in the broad windows.

A woman is in the kitchen with me.

"Dee."

I turn to look at her.

"You made it."

"Yes," I say, the words coming to me, unbidden. She looks a bit like Sandra, but younger. Darker skin.

"What do you think of the kitchen?"

"It's very nice. I love what you've done with it."

I feel like I'm on a recording, but not quite. I can still move …

I step over by the French doors. The backyard is

carefully landscaped; a small Buddha rests beneath a fruit tree. A stone bowl on a pedestal sports stone birds drinking from the pool of water. I look at the woman's face.

"What's your name?" I ask.

"You've forgotten."

"Yes."

"The doctors said this would happen."

"Yes, I'm sorry, honey."

"It's okay. Do you want breakfast?"

"Yes, please." I kiss her cheek. I go out on the patio, in the sun. The sheer unreality strikes me for a moment, but it passes. The light is beautiful, and warm. I sit in the wicker chair and contemplate the fruit trees and the chirping birds.

The woman is scrambling eggs, her smooth forearm whipping them in a metal bowl. She turns on the radio and a calm voice begins to announce the day's tragedies.

I know it isn't real. But what is real? It's real enough. An alien game …

"Breakfast," she says, smiling.

It is delicious. I pour Tabasco over the eggs and

scoop them onto my toast, wheat and hot. Sensory overload.

"Delicious," I say, and she smiles.

"I still don't remember your name." I try to smile.

"It's Sandra."

"Sandra, of course. When did I come back from the doctor?"

"Last week. Your memory has been improving. You should be proud!"

"Where are we?"

She stops smiling. "This is our home in Santa Barbara, John."

"It's a beautiful home."

"How are you feeling?"

"I feel fine. It's a lovely day."

"I'm going to need your help with the ant farm when you're finished with breakfast."

"Of course."

I wash the dishes in the sink. Every object, gleaming in the sunlight, seems hyperreal. Glowing in my mind. I dry the dishes and stack them in the glass-fronted cabinets.

I see the ant farm then, taking over the living room.

A huge nest of glass-fronted sand-passages, busily being milled by ants.

"The queen is angry," says Sandra, pointing to the center of the nest, a fishbowl-shaped area with lamps arranged around it to illuminate her bulbous, insectile glory.

"What's the matter?"

"She's figured out she's in a closed system."

"I see."

"The hive is suffering as a result. They knew already, but now that the queen knows, she's stopped reproducing. She's depressed."

"What do you want me to do?"

"Talk to her, Dee. Like you used to."

"I used to talk to ants?"

She takes my hand, and sits with me on "our" couch.

"Don't you remember, John? Try."

I try to think of something to say that will please her.

"I'll talk to her, honey."

"Thank you so much!" She kisses me, lightly, and heads back to the kitchen, putting on her music. I hunch down by the queen's lair.

"Hi, little devil," I say. "How's life in there?"

She regards me, I imagine, with heavy-lidded, fierce eyes.

"You gots to keep making babies, to make the queen mother happy. My queen mother. What do you say?"

The ant queen, not surprisingly, chooses not to reply in English.

I go out the front door, to look at American suburbia, this vanished biome.

It gleams and shines, like something from a propaganda film. Lazy vehicles glide by.

Dad?

What is it son.

Where are you?

On my trip. I told you.

I can't locate your position.

Don't worry. I'll be back.

Dad? I can't hear you.

Don't worry. Take care of Johnny. Take care of Semira.

… Dad

The rose garden is luxurious. Bursting with life. I step into it and feel the fecund heat of the bright plants, dark leaves, thick sun.

"Mr. Dee!" A man is on the sidewalk.

"Hello!" I say. I smile.

He hands me a manila envelope.

"You've been served," he says, and the smile falls off my face.

LAW OFFICES OF CHAIMOUGKOS reads the return address.

"Fuck."

F-16s fly over the sky.

I am American. I am this thing, called American. Though America is dead, I am American. Named for an improbable Italian.

America is dead but I am alive, American. What does it mean?

Why should I be this thing called American?

American man.

The sidewalks and the houses and the infrastructure of the personal internal combustion powered vehicle, ubiquitous iniquitous Americana rituals without name or need or end, I shall not surrender, though

I be in the midst of the shadow of the valley of American history, I shall not surrender.

I am Dee. My namesake John began the colonial empire that was Britain at its birth, sown from an improbable sea disaster, Spanish galleons hung with cannon and gold, sunk into the Channel, and my spirits, my familiars, hover over my shoulders, angels devils and small gods of all varieties, nature spirits and those beyond nature, tucked into the mailboxes and driveways of a Southern California that feels as though it never really existed, even in the midst of existing …

I am John Dee. I am American. I am being sued by an interdimensional alien. I am an avatar to save humanity. I am amnesiac schizophrenic manic-depressive magician, hero and villain, depending on your perspective …

I am a colonist. And I am a native.

Whatever. I hate being sued.

I go back inside. I show it to Sandra.

She shakes her head, her braids dancing around her face.

"We're going to go broke, Dee," she says.

"Probably." I kiss her.

❏

I'm remembering Texas. I was playing with my friends under a bridge—the water and sand rich with the smell of sewage.

Over the sky—no, that was later.

It was a clear day.

It would be better to forget. But that is what I'm recovering from. Whatever they did to me when I crossed the County Line … it's begun to fade.

We continue to imagine that the past is a settled thing, and that the future is uncertain, when the truth is that both are in flux, and we move in both directions at once …

I can see her face under that bridge, digging in the sand.

She knew something of what was to come. Why do women see the future more often than men?

❏

I'm sitting on the lawn. In Santa Barbara. There is a UFO hovering over my house. Humming. No, it is the lawnmower. My wife is mowing the lawn I'm sitting on. She is shouting at me.

The UFO is coming closer. My wife leans down, shouting into my face. She turns off the mower. Somewhere overhead I can hear the UFO shift its beam.

"You're supposed to be picking up our son!" she is shouting.

I climb into our SUV and drive. The satellite tells me where to go.

Our boy is dead but he has been revived.

One mile to go; I'm speeding.

We've had to update his software; he had been glitching. It was shameful. I remember this. I see him standing by the school, tears rolling down his face.

I pull up to the curb and throw open the passenger door. The warning chimes bleep at me from the dashboard.

"Get in!"

He climbs in, solemnly.

"Close the door!"

He does and the seatbelt crawls around him gently, securing him in place. I take off like a wildman back down the surburban curves.

"What did you learn in school today!" I shout, but he doesn't answer. He looks out the window.

I pull back up outside our beautiful house. My beautiful wife is mowing the lawn, sweating, like a Venusian goddess.

"Look at that woman mow that lawn," I say.

"Can we play Roman Castles?" he asks.

"After you do your homework."

"Teacher didn't give us any homework!"

"Yes she did. You always have homework."

"I did it in my head."

"Well, now do it on paper."

He detaches his belt and my wife embraces the boy when he gets out, her eyes on me. In a fit of pique I re-engage the engine and go hunting ice cream. Maraschino cherry.

□

It's bright red; cancerous. I watch the ice cream girl while I lick my cone.

Her eyes … they're like the boy who killed himself. I have to get out of here.

Dad?

Yeah, son.

Dad?

I'm here, son.

Dad?

I'm coming.

But not yet.

I drive into the hills. Overhead I see the Foo fighters circling. They're back! I knew it. I wave enthusiastically. Sticky ice cream in my moustache.

I know this life is a simulation. Life imitating art imitating life. My art is itself a simulation, copying patterns from a dimension unknown to us. Language is a simulation too. Chicken and egg . . .

No answers forthcoming today. I wave at the UFOs. They aren't real either. Or: they were real. But not here.

I am moving through space. Towards the aliens' prison planet, where my city's people have been relocated. Or so I believe.

What am I supposed to do?

◻

I make love to Sandra, who is not Sandra.

I will be a good pretend husband. And a good pretend father. In a beautiful pretend house. In a pretend city.

My pretend wife is cumming. So am I.

◻

The rosebushes are beautiful. I examine them on our front lawn, in the morning light.

The lawsuit! I had forgotten.

I bring the paper to the porch and light a cigarette, just to be an asshole. It's not real anyway! Hehehe. It reads:

CHAIMOUGKOS CORPORATION v
JOHN DEE

To wit:

John Dee, the lawful property of the information-alien state, has been resisting the lawful arrest of his brain.

This fiat asks all relevant forces of the universe to compell

Mr. Dee to submit to information processing, on penalty of death.

I laugh, and take a drag of my cigarette.

The hearing is this afternoon. Ought to be enough time to muster up a defense ... I was in model U.N., after all. I represented Djibouti.

Time for more coffee.

Maybe my argument should be that I'm not real, and therefore that any information gleaned from me would be useless to them anyway. But the question isn't really the efficacy of the information, just that it exists, and they want it ...

Is real information different from unreal information?

More coffee.

Now clearly it should be that they can't own my thoughts. Even though they own my "body" in this subordinate information system, those things occuring "inside" of "me" are "mine" in any reasonable ethical framework . . .

A simple anti-mind-control argument. Ironic given that I'm a professional mind-controller ...

I get in my car and drive. They're judging America; I see that now. Or at least Los Angeles. Or maybe judgment isn't the right word for it . . .

I step down on the accelerator.

The slow curve of the road soothes me. I can see the arguments flowing off my tongue in court ... positive visualization, Dee!

I am a worthwhile and dignified human being. I am the light of awareness of my own body. I am useful, and competent. I have good friends. I have a beautiful wife. I have a dead son. I myself have been revivified. I own a strong, shiny and useful automobile. My city has been constructed for my amusement and convenience. The galaxy beckons . . .

The golden orb . . .

What right have I to know.

What ludicrous expression of divinity is this, writing. What hole in space ...

I am a magician. I attend to the flux in awareness, the stirring of the bomb of light ...

I park the car. I tighten my tie. I tip the robot valet.

"Give it a shine, will you, Jimmy?" His red eyes glimmer.

Outside the Chaimougkos Hotel slash Courtoom.

Its tentacles rise into the sky. Spotlights move around its phallic skyscraper body.

I open the doors.

A huge and comical voice, basso profundo, intones:

"Welcome to Court. Please leave your weapons at the door."

Brass knuckles. Stun gun. Forty-five. Laser sight. My garotte. Hmm, what else …

"Let the accused come forward!"

The room is vast, in dim light. Shadows and colors move in the enormous darkness.

I have a beautiful wife. I have a beautiful house. I have a mind control device. I am a useful and respected member of society. I am a magician. I am the father of a young boy. I possess many unusual skills. People like me.

"Your name?" the voice intones.

"Dee. I'm Dee."

"Welcome, Dee. I am your interlocutor. Do you require refreshment?"

"Got any whiskey?"

"A drink for the magician."

A small robot produces a tray with a jelly glass. I

swirl the brown liquid under my nose, standing on the plush carpet in the dimness.

"Forgive the lighting, John Dee. I am not accustomed to the brightness your people enjoy. Do you understand why you have been summoned here?"

"Not really."

The Voice pauses a moment. The little server robot watches me.

"Really I just want to talk to you, Dee. I want you to help me understand you. Are you comfortable?"

"I'm great. What do you want to know?"

"What is it like to be a man?"

"Well, you're tired all the time. Confused most of the time. Beleaguered and put upon and pursued and thwarted, but other than that it's pretty good."

"Yes, we understand the confusion. We are confused too. We need you to do something for us, John Dee. It should be easy for you."

"I'm all ears, scary voice in the dark."

"Are we so scary?"

"What do you want me to do?"

"When you get … where you're going. There's a man—well, he looks like a man—who lives in an old carriage. You're familiar with carriages?"

"Uh huh."

"He lives in one of them. We need you to visit him. And tell him, that his services, are to be rewarded."

"Great. Can do, boss. Now: you mind telling me how to wake up from this nightmare?"

"You're doing so well, Dee. Keep going. We love watching you."

The "presence" receded into the darkness, and it grew quiet. Somewhere in the dimness, I heard a cricket.

I stormed back outside, gave my ticket to the robot, and drove home.

◻

I drink my whiskey in my den, with my wife on my lap.

"Dad?" asks our dead son, standing in the hall.

"What is it son?"

"I want a bed time story."

"Be right there."

"I want a bed time story too," my wife says.

You may find yourself in a beautiful house, with a beautiful wife, and ask yourself, how did I get here?

"Once upon a time, in zombie land," I tell my son, "there was a huge house, that looked over a cliff."

"They built it on a cliff?"

"Yes. And everyone in the village was afraid to go into this house, because they said it was haunted. But a boy in the village, a boy about your age, one day decided to venture up to the cliff, and he opened the door to the house, and went inside.

"Inside the house there was a beautiful dead woman, though the boy didn't know she was dead at first, because she had on a white wedding dress, and had shining white hair. 'Wouldn't you like some fruit, boy?' she asked, holding out to the boy a glowing, fragrant object. 'No thank you,' said the boy."

"What was the boy's name?"

"Johnny. And Johnny looked closely at the dead woman's face and saw a whole galaxy inside of it, spinning around in her face, and that's when the little boy realized he had to leave his village, for the whole of it was haunted. And he did, the next Spring. He enlisted as an apprentice juggler with the journeyman

81

juggler who came through, and he never returned to his home or to the haunted house until he was very much older."

"He came back?"

"Yes, he came back. He'd had a great many adventures but had never married, nor had any children, and he believed the haunting of his village was to blame, so he returned with the intention of banishing the ghost. And that was what he set out to do when he visited the village priest. And that's all for tonight."

"Dad!"

"Go to sleep."

□

I tell my wife another story, with my body, but I fear neither is enough for what is coming; what I have come to do.

□

I see now the conundrum: I am like the ant queen

in the ant farm. Aware of the limitations of my world but unable to do anything about it. Except refuse to act.

Perhaps there is some clue in the structure of suburbia itself: the green grass invites one to believe one is in a natural environment, while the sturdy house invites feelings of civilization, while all the while the automobile system, with its roads, machines of death, and destruction of the environment accelerates apace, sucking suburbanites in to "work," a process they hope to be divorced from reality itself . . .

My own "imprisonment" here is not so different. Except that I am embarked on a journey of salvation. But perhaps those who designed the internal combustion engine and drilled the oil believed so too.

The sun watches over me, and the white houses glow, and I sip my martini, plotting my next move . . .

What'll it be, gumshoe? The frying pan, or the fire?

◻

As though I'm on a boat: America. Through a winter sea. Sailing . . .

Sailing ...

Lights outside my window. My wife is up on the roof, performing salutations to the sun. The fire engines glide down the street.

My dead son is running down the sidewalk.

Towards the haunted house.

At the end of the block.

On the edge of the cliff.

No one may know me, but—

I know you, Dad. WHAT THE HELL ARE YOU DOING?

No one may know me, but I know me. I go down the stairs.

I open the door and go back out onto the sidewalk.

The red roses are gleaming, fires, upon fires ...

I run after the dead boy, my imaginary son, in the world called America, in a time both irreparable and potential, my feet slapping asphalt, the boy's laughter, rising over the mid-morning humidity, the sprinklers (my shoes are getting wet!), the UFOs, and the house on the cliff with the dead woman inside ...

Lemmings are throwing themselves over the cliff. A huge Pied Piper mob. I made through the crazed mammalian bodies, looking for the bobbing head of my son, moving towards the sepulcher that is the ghost's shelter, the Victorian spires twisting in the light …

"Johnny!"

He turns to look and the mob overtakes him, lemming bodies swarming him, carrying him as over a mosh-pit, twisting, and turning, bubbling bodies, I push harder through them, and I will the world,

I will the world,

I will the world,

With all that I am:

With all that I am:

Yes, Dee?

Give me back my son.

Is that what you want, Dee?

Yes. Make him alive again.

It'll cost you.

Do it.

The tide ebbs.

UFOs hover over the haunted house.

The lemmings push to their death but my son is out of the mob now, running to the porch …

"Stop!"

But he's already inside.

Every Russian doll carries a story …

□

If I know what wind is blowing, will I know what it is? It has no cardinal direction, but one of the mind.

□

I follow the boy up the stairs. In this world I know my boy died by eletrocution, in a house fire; he's a bit jerky because of it.

The world behind the world, underneath the world.

I pursue the boy and the house pursues me. I understand that it is The Great House. But this is no matter, great or not, still a house. A large container for spirits. A grand temple for gods. A chieftain's hut. The Earth.

I am inside a great man, The Earth, temple and chieftain. I am a bacterium, pursuing another, within our great road. While the Wizardess pursues us both, her white locks shining in the half-light of the suns within the hallways—the solar lamps.

I turn the corner upstairs, and the boy is laughing, and slips through a door, shutting it behind him, and I knock, shouting:

What do I shout. Some words I can't understand. Open up, perhaps. Open up, son, it's your father, come to kill you. It's Daddy, come to save you. Jahweh, holding an iron brand, to mark you.

The door opens and he is within, possessed by spirits and I kneel before him without thinking, his white eyes glowing, and I speak his name, and then he hugs me, laughing, and opens the secret door in his bedroom down into the basement:

Beneath The Great House, the Great Basement.

Beneath the temple, the ruins.

Beneath the Earth, the aether.

Down into the basement.

"It's okay, Dad," the boy says, leading me down the stairs, his white eyes glowing.

"You remind me of my son," I tell him.

"I am!" he says, and I smile, crossing myself, though

that is only a vestigial gesture. If I worship any gods, they are alive.

We move into the sepulchers and basements, our oldest ancestors' worlds, cave ruins and pits, charnel houses of bodies, bones, and spirits, where the real work gets done …

Where Caesar gets approval for his war on Gaul. Where the Hierophants seek license for their magic spells. Where armies are rejuvenated, underneath corridors of sky, in corridors of Man:

"I love you, Dad," the boy says, his eyes glowing brighter.

"And I you, son."

In the basement I am imprisoned.

Shackled to the wall, and the boy begins to note my reactions, a good scientist.

Torture is merely a turning. Time brings in more than revenges: it brings change. Like a fresh lake born from a hurricane.

I answer all his questions truthfully, and I lie. And I scream. I know these notebooks are my own. Something I made.

In the basement of the reality I knew, I set certain

charges to allow myself to survive these next events … so all men must do, when driven to the knowledge brought by extremes.

My small city far away, City of Messengers, bearing their cane papyri, priests of all nations, sprinters and endurance runners, setting the scales turning, of our world.

But I know I am talking too much.

In the dream world of the aliens, I learned many things which are ultimately untranslatable. Be assured that enough of me survived to deliver this statement (though it is possible I wrote some of it before I left and misremember).

I who was Dee—in name only, in many ways—became him more deeply during and after the torture by my imaginary son in an imaginary basement I had created, a basement which represented (and was) the foundation of human religion.

Superstition is a term I continue to enjoy using to describe religion because of its literal quality: a standing over. Superstition and religion is a profound acknowledgement, implicitly, of all that lies beneath it: the basement, and the Earth.

Another way of saying: "well, here we are."

Here I am. Los Angeles, my love.

Sandra.

J'arrive ma puce! I will be a knight sans armor.

I serve you.

And I serve you, reader. Whoever you are. May your efforts yet redeem me, who have damned myself on your behalf.

□

I awoke in orbit around Alpha Centauri—First Horseman. Of the Apocalypse, if you like. Or of the invasion. The tentacles withdrew themselves from my skull aboard the interstellar dreamship and I was overcome with the sensation of having failed. I know, of course, that I did, whatever I will say later.

The tentacled ones put me in a pod and fired me towards the surface of their planet, in orbit about the bright Horseman Sun.

I was mad. I am mad now. But my madness then, unlike now, was still a new thing, and it frightened me, with the rage against everything my actions would soon become, and with the immediacy of my senses. Whatever else it is, madness is a powerful drug that awakens the mind and fires the senses—the eyes in particular—to life.

I crashed into the ocean and managed to tear out of my pod before it sank completely. I was not found for two days. In that time afloat I concocted a plan— one I'm still rather proud of—to rescue the people of that strange world. I would have to, for their own good, subdue the planet to my will.

Is it any wonder that dictators are brought to power again and again in human history? So rarely are enough willing to fight them. And people want to be told.

Arise!

Liberate this world!

Let none stand in your way!

◻

Everything I was is gone but I will pretend otherwise.

In truth there are now at least two Dees: the Dee

who went and returned, and the Dee who never left. They are two and separate people, though they live in the same body. I see them in ongoing negotiation. Or perhaps it is that one has already conquered the other, without the conquered realizing it. And I do not know for certain which is telling this tale. Perhaps they agreed to tell it together.

I who tell this story am you too. Forgive me. I wish it were a better story. I wish you were here to tell it too. Though I killed you, Dee.

Tell me it was worth it. That all I have done has some meaning. To be otherwise would be too painful.

Even if it is not so I believe it. That my struggle was yours too, and though I undertook my travails voluntarily I did it at your bidding, and that many of my gravest sins were for your sake.

It could be so. But you, of course, must judge.

◻

I met John Lake shortly after my rescue. I was brought on their skiff to his village and given shelter to recover from my spell at sea.

To say his support was invaluable to my efforts to take control of Horseman would be an understatement: for so many reasons he was the catalyst to my plans, electrifying what would otherwise have been but callow efforts to inspire his people.

"You are an alien here," he said to me.

"Yes."

"Many will be afraid."

"Are you afraid?"

"Yes."

I held his hand.

"Many things have happened on our homeworld. I need your help."

"Tell me."

It is a truism that new arrivals are gifted with their anonymity, and may be princes if they wish—no one can naysay them. Royalty is one's bearing, you know. When many believe, it is so.

I became royalty for John, because that was what they needed. Perhaps I needed it too. We took the continent within days.

◻

The festivals at night were beautiful, over the lagoons, with the fireworks. I lay in my boat with my woman and sucked on the hookah, filled with their native herbs, watching the lights play over the stilted houses of the marshland.

I have been elected president. Leader of 5,000.

I promised them dominion over their neighboring continents, a promise I said would be easy for me to deliver as I have favored relations with the tentacled ones, in orbit. All this is nonsense, of course. But the election was fine, and this celebration is finer, wrapped in the heat of the night, with a beautiful woman watching me delight in their childlike celebrations.

"Are you aware of where we're going?" she asked me.

"No," I said, and smiled. "Wherever it is, it must be beautiful."

"It is," she said, smiling in a strange way. "So beautiful."

❏

I believe I know now why Los Angeles left. They had been hoping for this day to come: union with the aliens. They are no longer human, though they look it.

I have been put in prison. It's pleasant enough—it reminds me of my old apartment. It looks, in fact, a great deal like it. Perhaps they scanned my memories.

The view from my window is of a simulated Koreatown. My gaoler is knocking:

"What do you want?" I shout through the door.

"Your lunch."

He hands me the sandwich and leaves. He disappears down the corridor. I have tried the stairwell to the ground floor but it is blocked with some kind of forcefield.

The woman had given me a drug. They'd left me a note, when I awoke on the bed of this cell:

"Don't be so sure you know what's best for us. You have been sentenced to five years."

Part of me was almost grateful. The release from responsibility. The other part of me has begun planning my escape.

Dad?

Yeah son.

Where are you?

I don't know. Wherever these goddamned aliens have put me.

I'm coming to find you.

Thanks kid.

◻

I'm sorry Los Angeles. I've failed you.

◻

It's something inside. Maybe we put it there ourselves. Inside the tectonic zone. Something horrible. Beautiful. Ecstatic. Something I have no name for, Los Angeles.

I don't have enough, not yet. Not enough information. Not enough time. My memories—not enough of them functional either.

I have you son.

I'm coming, Dad.

I have—had—Semira. Even though she's dead.

I have you. Whoever you are.

I have myself. I have this terrible dream of Los Angeles, my prison.

I hate you, prison.

And I will liberate you.

There is nothing more painful than liberation. I who have been tortured can attest to this. Even torture has an end. But freedom is without end.

◻

To understand a simulation you must acquire a reference point. It is helpful to have some knowledge of theater. Who are they referencing? What tropes, and what dividends? What subject, and what license? What intent. What theme, and low ribald drip, muscular spectacular, flows like thorazine into the mind...

Perception itself is a kind of thorazine, made to reduce the valve. What do my gaolers want me to know? And what not?

If I die in this prison, will I awake?

As a magician I understand that it is dangerous to

97

play with perception—many decisions you make with your eyes, ears and brain can be irreversible. So one does not alter one's perceptions without good reason.

Open the door, baby. (And let the aliens in—)

◻

My shadow self.

Hovering over my head, like a demon.

Hello, Dee.

HELLO

Well, what's it going to be?

THE ALIENS IN ORBIT, CAN YOU SEE THEM?

Him with his beard and his plague mask.

No Dee, I can't see them. Can you?

YES

Give me a trajectory.

RAISE YOUR HAND

I raise my hand, making from my fingers a child's gun, index finger pointed.

TWENTY-FIVE ARC-SECONDS BELOW THE TOP OF THAT FLOOD LIGHT ATOP THE SHOP-PING CENTER OUTSIDE YOUR WINDOW, DEE

I see it.

FIRE ON MY MARK.

I raise my hand.

FIRE DEE

I pull the trigger. Shooting the orbital out of the sky. Fire from my heart

YES

Storming out of the sky

Burning in the light

The explosion has shut off the forfield at the stair.

I run down.

Into the empty streets.

The burning is in the distance. I'm running.

I AM WITH YOU

I hate you, Dee.

I KNOW. PRISON ISN'T EASY DEE

You're telling me, you fucking spook. Where the fuck am I?

YOU'RE IN THE ALIENS' SIMULATION.

Where am I physically?

IN SEDATION. ON THEIR COLONY. YOU MUST LIBERATE LOS ANGELES DEE. BRING THEM BACK.

Fuck me.

GLADLY

He skirts around me, like an afterimage shock. I sweep around my head with my hands, still running, like trying to ward off flies.

HE HE HE

The aliens are burning.

SHOOT THEM DEE

I raise my hand.

SHOOT THEM

One of them raises its hand.

SHOOT THEM!

I lower my hand.

GODDAMN IT DEE!

I approach the downed UFO.

"How you doing brother?"

"You shot us down."

Its voice sounds like plague. Perhaps we are the plague.

"You know you're in a simulation, right?"

"Kill me." It reaches for my hand.

"I'm here to liberate you," I say.

"You killed my friends," it says.

"But I didn't kill you. My self wanted to."

"What?"

"My other self."

"How did you see through our cloaking device?"

"With the help of my friend."

"Your other self."

"Would you take off your helmet, please?"

The alien does and darkness spills out of it, like a dark ichor, pooling around its feet, over the empty LA asphalt.

"Just kidding, put it back on please."

"Help me clean up this fucking mess."

◻

Fires are burning in the city. Jimmy and I (I call the crashed alien that) have found some welding gear and are disassembling his craft. He doesn't appear to need food. I take breaks to heat up chili but he just keeps on cutting. It'll probably take two more days.

The city is beautiful when empty. Like a well thought out tomb, with every sepulcher artfully decorated and arranged.

"Let me give you a hand with that, Jimmy." I help him carry a part of the heat shield to the heap. "Are you sure you don't want to bury your buddies?" He's left them lying in the wreckage.

"You can stop assisting me any time you like." His voice is clipped, far away.

"Sorry."

When night falls I go looking for the fires. More crash landings? Smoke is rising over Hollywood.

To understand a simulation one must understand the reference point. What story am I in, Dee?

YOU'RE IN AN ADVENTURE STORY

Hmm. Do I have a goal within this simulation?

VICTORY

Ha ha ha! That clears everything up for me. Who am I supposed to be victorious over?

THE ALIENS!

Which ones?

I DON'T KNOW

I wear my Dee as a cloak, my familiar myself. What else can I do within this simulation?

Los Angeles wants to stay Los Angeles. Los Angeles wants to stay in Los Angeles. But Los Angeles has gone away, and I followed. And now they've trapped me in a simulated Los Angeles, on a faraway world . . .

The narrative arc of Los Angeles must have been translated then too, into this scheme. Who does the city want to be. What triumphs does it want. Who are its enemies, its heroes.

YOU DEE

Tell me its enemies then, goddamn it!

YOU TOO

◻

It's as though I'm back where I started except now everything is a lie. I'm sleeping in my sewer, sans Semira. Just little old Dee, and his trusty ghosts . . .

I've got a lock on you Dad

Is that you son?

I'm closing in. They made it really hard to find you
. . .

I drink the water from the tap and go through the manhole to the surface. Jimmy has almost dismanted the craft. The bodies of his compatriots still lie there, in their bright red metal suits. I help him drag the last cut up pieces to the heap.

"What now Jimmy?"

"Tell me something, Dee. Just what are you doing here?"

"You got me, Jimmy. They don't tell me anything. What are you doing here?"

"I was flying. We're a scoutship. You shot us down … they told us to expect resistance but we hadn't seen any signs of violent life, until you showed up."

"Let me make it up to you, Jimmy. Hmm? What can I do?"

"Let me scan you."

"Sure, fine."

Jimmy comes closer to me. I can see my own bearded face reflected in his glassy visor.

"It's not as easy as it sounds. It could kill you."

"That would be fine with me."

"It's not that I want to kill you. But if the scanner provides an intelligible result, it could justify the loss of the ship to homeworld. Do you consent?"

"Do me, Jimmy, okay? Sounds fun."

"Hold still."

23

Genre police, in your Nazi craft, in your low regard for the truth, fly with me, and I will show you something different, from the sky, or the earth, I will fly within you, to the truth:

No truth but within, inside the grin of our hearts...

Genre police, karma police, you cycling madmen of the deep, come with me.

Beyond this country. Beyond the flesh we know. No logos reigns supreme at scales inaccessible to Man:

24

Scanned

In Texas I was a boy.

Define boy for us.

I was young. Boy means human male, prior to sexual maturity. I lived with my mother under a bridge … no, that isn't right. We visited the bridge. It smelled of chemicals; the oil companies dumped their waste upstream. But the sand was fun to play in.

You are made out of oil?

Umm, no. But the same constituent elements, yes.

What was this bridge?

It was in a county park. Just a small bridge. A patch of sand, by the chemical water. We played there, my friends and I.

What are friends?

Other people, not related directly to me. Neighbors. People we knew.

What are neighbors?

Other people who lived nearby.

Why did you do this?

For fun. It was fun, the sand.

Explain this ceremony.

I can see Jimmy hovering there, under the bridge. Floating in the air in the afternoon light.

My friend Alan sees him too.

"Hey, an alien!" He laughs.

"It's my friend," I find myself saying.

We're manipulating your memories, Dee, just so you understand. Please forgive the intrustion.

"Alan, they want to know what kind we are."

"Is he real? Hey, are you real!" Alan says.

Jimmy fades. But I feel him hovering.

We go home. I eat broccoli and canned peaches with Alan and my mom. Later me and Alan play Castle. In bed that night, I see Jimmy's face, hovering over my bed . . .

We're fast forwarding . . .

◻

Identity is both an aggregate of experience and some deeper waveform, resistant to the exigencies of life after life, obdurate, again and again:

Sun is rising in England. I am a university student.

My girlfriend is holding my hand, after a rain.

I'm in bed with her.

I can feel Jimmy hovering at the level of the ceiling.

We're punting—in the boat on the Thames—in the early summer light. Jimmy is in the boat with us.

I pull the oars.

I'm on a train. With my college friends. Heading into Paris.

This is before I was a magician, I realize. Before everything changed.

What is a magician, Dee?

A man. A crazy man.

An outcast, you mean.

If you like.

I'm with Semira. When I shot her.

You didn't shoot her, Dee.

I'm shooting her.

You're not.

This is later. What are you looking for, Jimmy?

We see it.

Semira is laughing. Laughing and laughing. Dancing

in her red, in the Silver Lake hills.

This is about the Church, isn't it, Jimmy? The Church of S.

In part. We believe it's connected to why you shot down our craft. Why you could see us.

Who are you, Jimmy?

Just another alien. Relax into the scan.

Over Silver Lake, a UFO is rising from the water. The same water where I killed a man. So long ago it seems like now.

Dee, what is your purpose?

Dunno.

I'm running. Running in the alleys of Los Angeles. But what happened before, Jimmy? Why did I become a magician?

We don't know. When did you become outcast?

I don't know!

25

Jimmy

The scan is over. Jimmy takes the scanner off my body and puts it back in his metal pocket.

"What did you find, Jimmy?"

"Some things. Come on, we're going to bury my friends now."

▫

"Do you know much about ancient Rome, Dee?"

"I don't know, Jimmy. Why do you ask?"

We're arranging the sepulcher, putting the transmitters in their array—little silver boxes.

"What do you believe religion is, Dee?"

"Just the stuff people do."

I can feel Jimmy smiling, though I can't see his face.

"What do you think we're doing now, Dee?"

"This gonna teleport em out of here and shit?"

"We're going to teleport you, Dee. To my home-world."

"Great."

"Are you ready?"

"Hit me, Jimmy."

I am light.

Beam me up, motherfucker!

Beam me up, you cowardly motherfucker!

Who are you talking to, Dee?

You! Whoever the fuck you are!

Part 2

Homeworld

26

Light

I am on Homeworld.

My princess takes me back into her boat. I have passed the test—the ghosts have entered my brain.

We are conquering the continent.

I feel like a robot, a little bit. But I know it's more than that. Various levels of reality have coalesced in my body. I am not to blame for that.

That must have been what happened to Los Angeles—some kind of confluence of equations—yielding an autonomous state of matter . . .

"You look beautiful."

She has put the crown atop my head.

I smile. I know it is a frightening expression.

◻

I am watching myself from some distance. As I said, the people (the human colonists) of Homeworld want me as their avatar, their central point—the figurehead. But as I enact the role of figurehead I feel myself slipping away. I watch my body do things, and my mouth speak words I would not have said.

I am watching from a distance, down within.

I lurk in my heart, as we:

Ride over the aliens in our skiffs, firing shadows into their eyes, their bodies falling to the earth, netted by black twisting forms. (Perhaps Jimmy was a victim of mine? Or future victim . . .)

We cross the sea, artillery preceding us, my men and women armed and armoured, brilliant in the light and the cold, and part of me orders orbital bombardment. I am a vessel—a machine.

Take me, and take with me, your city, your city is dying—take me, with your city. I am yours, whatever I am now is yours. Take me.

The Travelers from their ship in orbit fire the nest seeds and the chromatic fungi fall from the sky, infesting the air, killing thousands of the enemy. We ride through in our gas masks, killing retail: one blade, for one heart.

I massacre the inhabitants of the continent.

Our thousand genocides exist within our heart,

separating, and coalescing, as a fluid:

My blood too.

I am screaming, victor.

And watching from far away.

One of the women comes to my bed. And then a second.

Over us the Travelers are watching.

In my prison, in the false Los Angeles, some part of me was removed … I do not know. I must regain control of my body.

WE'RE WAITING DEE

What do I do.

WAKE UP.

Blood on my hands. And cum.

The women's greedy eyes on me.

I want to remember nothing.

REMEMBER DEE

I don't want to.

PLEASE

Who are you?

WE ARE YOUR SERVANTS DEE. PLEASE

I rise in my tent.

"Leave me," I say to the women. "Bring me the

commander."

In a moment he is standing outside my tent, uncertain. He sees the different look in my eyes.

"I'm done now. You can continue the war if you like. Or if you will still follow me, declare the war over."

"What do you mean, Emperor?"

"My name is Dee. Call me that."

"Yes, Emperor. But the natives are coming in a second wave—we've sighted them at seven klicks out. We should be able to annihilate them with another orbital launch if your friends are willing."

"Please, remind me of your name."

"Ben, highness."

"Ben. Tell me, would you, who is our contact with the natives?"

"Contact? We have none, Emperor."

"Please, come in. Let me make you tea."

"Let me serve you, highness."

"No, let me. Sit."

I make the tea.

"I have been unwell. My memory, it has gaps."

"You are brave, Emperor."

2 DEE

"Please, call me Dee. I want to parlay with the enemy. Do we have a craft that can project my voice to them, from a safe distance?"

"Let me parlay, Emperor. What do you want to say?"

"We will go to together."

"As you say. I will bring a contingent to counter-attack if they become hostile."

"They are already. As are we. Bring no contingent. We must make peace."

◻

Over the bright eaves of the forest canopy the sun is rising. I can see the enemy's smoke in the distance. Our skiff hums.

"You'll be in hailing distance in ten seconds," Ben says.

I raise the microphone to my lips. I hold my thumb over the transmit button.

"This translator is up to date?" I ask.

"We'll find out."

I press the button and open my mouth.

YOU'RE A GREAT MAN DEE

Shut up

"Aliens. Natives. People of Homeworld. I knew your Jimmy. I called him Jimmy."

"They're loading a missile right now, lord," Ben whispers in my ear.

"I am the Emperor of this planet. I want peace. Please, let us land at your camp. We will not fire."

"That missile is loaded and tracking us, lord."

I can hear the translated echoes of my speech echo over the forest air. In the distance I see a small drone lift above the trees. It begins to speak, its speaker crackling in the most air.

"It's telling us to land, lord."

We go in, down under the leaves.

◻

I've found you Dad.

I'm kind of busy now son.

Getting really close . . .

Their faces peer up at our craft, yellow eyes liquid in the light and smoke. We settle down and I open the door, smelling the fear—from both our tribes.

"This is my sidearm," I say, into the translator, while holding out my gun. "Will you accept it?"

One of the natives watches me and speaks. The translator remains silent.

Another native comes and takes my gun. And he offers me his rifle, glowing low and red. I take it in my hand and it tingles.

The first native, with greener yellow eyes, speaks again. This time it is translated, in the box's scratchy voice:

"You have killed whole tribes of our people. But we can't overome your friends in the sky. What kind of being are you who slaughters so thoughtlessly?"

"I am a human being. From Earth, far away. My ancestors in Greece would exchange weapons as we have done. To make peace. I'm glad the custom appears the same with you."

The box crackles again, translating the native's speech: "We have no choice. Come, and eat with us."

They serve us fried insects. They are delicious.

The red rifle is glowing in my lap.

I smile, and bite into another centipede.

❏

Whatever it was is not gone—that faraway feeling. I watch it come back as we dance with the natives, hearing their strange music. One of the Travelers has come to a much lower altitude. We can see its eyes above the canopy.

I dance around the fire. Whoever I am.

I'm here Dad.

"How ya doin son!"

I pound the earth with my feet. I hold hands with Ben, and then with a native. I shake my hair.

I have information for you, Dad.

"What is it son!"

Los Angeles is disappearing.

I grin wider. I am not a thinking being—not now. I'm just a dancer.

My AI son Albert shimmers in the air, flickering the natives' torches. They smile to see the ghost. They know it for mine.

□

The green-yellow eyed one I've taken to calling Stug bids me follow him into his forest, the morning after our night of dancing. He is speaking in his language, heavy with glottal stops. The translator spits out words:

"Every tree has a name. We've given you a name too, which we may not tell you. We knew the Travelers were coming. Tell me, why did you come here?"

"My city was kidnapped. The trail led me here."

"We do not have cities here, but we have seen photographs. Isn't it possible that your city fled, of its own free will?"

"That's possible, yes. Indeed, that's what I had assumed had happened—that they had gone to another of our planets, Mars. Perhaps our city is a prison, as you are implying. But if so, I am its gaoler. I must return our citizens to their rightful home."

"And now you are Emperor here. You can have many mates, and much food, and we are your friends, of necessity. Still, you would wrench these people out of their homes, and put them back aboard the Travelers?"

"Wouldn't you like me to do that, Stug?"

"You are wise to call me that. I could kill you now, you know. And that might be wise too. Tell me, if you are the gaoler of this prison city, who is the warden?"

"I don't know."

"Perhaps I would like to meet this warden."

"Perhaps I would too."

□

Far away in light, I remember. I remember my city. And Semira. She's still there. I'm sure she's found enough drugs—the dealers have remained, hoarding their stockpiles. I remember my travels. And Foo, where is he? Has he abandoned us?

Dad

Yes son.

I think we have a problem.

What is it son.

Ben is being taken prisoner.

I slip my knife out of my sleeve and hold it against Stug's throat. His bright yellow eyes bore into mine.

"Little man. Get on your knees."

I tie his hands behind his back. I march him in front of me, my red pulsating alien rifle slung over my back.

◻

"Stug, what are your plans?"

"We will kill all of you."

"Why haven't you done it yet?"

"The gods must be propitiated."

"You mean the Travelers?"

"Those are foreign gods. We propitiate our own."

"A nice little human sacrifice."

"No. We will attach him to the Wheel."

"You'll torture him."

"Worse than torture. We will make him into a god."

The yellow sunlight, before so inviting, now seems alien. Burning the jungle and my skin.

If I was meant to be this, what could that mean?

"I still want to be your friend, Stug."

"I want to eat your corpse."

▫

I approach the village.

Three men, in the hut. Four, around the edges. You're approaching one now. Twenty meters.

"I've got your chief!" the words come from my throat, unbidden.

Then Stug shouts:

"Turn it on now!" He turns to me. "Now there's nothing you can do for your friend."

The Wheel is spinning Ben around. I fire my rifle at its control box, but the machine appears to absorb the round round, which only spins faster, leaking light.

The villagers are in a strange moment of peace.

"What is it doing Stug?"

"Making him a god."

"How do I stop it?"

"You don't."

Then Ben makes a horrible sound, and I fall to my knees. One of the other villagers comes and cuts Stug's bonds.

"You have a new friend now, Dee. May he bring you much pain."

Then he speaks to his villagers and the box does not translate.

From the dessicated corpse that was Ben a colored ghost is flowing out, over the rooves of the village, and over my head.

You fucked up Dad

How many ghosts do I need.

The villagers have vanished into the trees. I stare at the dirt. Over my head, I can feel Ben watching me.

I climb back into the skiff and program a return flight to my army.

Above the treeline, I see the Traveler lower its tentacles. Stug and his villagers are climbing aboard.

Ben flies next to me. Purple red and yellow, and filled with hate. And something else...

◻

Each decision we make narrows the range of possible decisions that follow it—but there is no end to decisions, or even their number. Perhaps I am wrong. Perhaps I only want to believe the course I'm on is inevitable. If I have no choice—or very little—I'll never have to figure out where it is I'm going.

27

Princess

She's in the shower. If I were a different man I would burrow down here, make arrangements and deals and attract followers, assemble arms, woo philosophers, charlatans, builders and diplomats from far regions all to keep a woman like this, to please her whims. Perhaps—likely—this is the kind of man she expects.

What is Los Angeles compared to this far kingdom?

And what is Semira compared to this princess?

What gum on my shoe stuck to my heart.

I go outside into the small city.

Overhead, Ben is vomiting red fire, like children's tricks.

Are you there son?

I'm here Dad.

I love you son.

I know Dad.

What do I do now, son?

Save the city, Dad.

I knew I had to do something. But what if the city doesn't want to be saved?

Save them anyway Dad.

But then what would "save" mean?

They don't know what they're missing Dad. You have to remind them.

"My people!" I shout. Some of them turn to look. Hardly an Emperor. More a glorified fishmonger.

"My people, listen."

What am I saving them from, son?

Themselves, Dad.

"My people, listen! We must undertake now a great journey. One not unlike the great journey that took you here, and that some of you have forgotten. I know some of you are saying that, with the enemy defeated, the planet is now ours. That we can thrive as the chiefs and lords of this continent, and others, and grow strong, and rich.

"Even if this were true—and it isn't—but even if it were true it would not be enough for you, my people. You are the people of Los Angeles. And this is not your home. I want you to come back. Los Angeles needs you. It's dying."

"What about the water!" someone shouts.

"There will be water for everyone!" I shout back. I have no idea how much water there is.

"The aliens, they'll eat us!" shouts an old Korean lady.

"I have made arrangements with them!" I shout back.

"Fuck your arrangements!"

Clearly I am no Ezekiel. How the hell did he ever get the Jews to leave Babylon?

I go to a cafe I like and order a sandwich. Fresh fried sea creature, of unknown origin.

I could just go back, alone. But then, why did I come? Can't I just leave them here, son?

You can do whatever you like, Dad.

I need a good propagandist.

Elizabeth was first motivated to Empire by John Dee. What did he say to her?

My people are alien to me now. More even than the natives here, who are a different species. Something about the light here reveals them—redder than their native Los Angeles. And their movements, the way they carry themselves, have grown foreign too. They don't hunch together and stand like birds, waiting for buses, or bow and twist around one another in subways like angry ants in a hive. They stand alone, watching their broad city on their broad continent, entirely their own.

The train of empire needs loading Dee. Pick up the shovel. Punch the tickets. Prepare the whistle, to blow:

❑

The princess moves underneath me like a slippery creekbed, winding her way towards some truth I can't see. Each woman changes a man in the instant of meeting her—or at least it is so for me. I am too vulnerable to them.

I whisper in her ear. I give her my body. Her eyes promise me that all I suspect of her motives and plans is true, that she will betray me at any moment, if she believes the advantage good enough.

❑

I hire the finest propagandist I can find—an art still new to this colony. Ahmed advises small perturbations in the daily fabric of the lives of his city's inhabitants—nothing too loud, or gauche. Each detail should be lovingly curated he says, like an art project. Like a grand party for a duchess. Sequins for my spoiled princess …

Ahmed's hairy arms reassure me somehow, believing as I do that propaganda is a fundamentally aggressive art. He will do what needs to be done.

I set out into our jungle. Just me and my ghosts.

28

Jungle

Pieces of the concrete jungle I've left behind come to me in flashes as I wind between the great trees. Graffiti and the obstreperous trainside plants, poking their noses between creosote and algae. A thousand miles of barbed wire. I miss it.

A bird has been following me overhead. Perhaps he likes my ghosts. He is red, like Ben, but a more beautiful shade. A real jungle bird, but with human-like eyes.

The trees are watching too. What have I done to this world? In defending Los Angeles, my many crimes … too many to number, perhaps.

If I place the defense of my city as my highest good, what will I be willing to do in its name? Destroy everything else? And if I were to do such a thing, would the city still be worthy of my defense? Would it still be a good place?

Are you there son?

Yes.

How many Travelers are in orbit?

Now? None.

Where did they go?

I don't know. Do you want me to find out?

Find Sandra. I've been procrastinating. Too long.

You need to do something for me first, Dad.

Anything, son.

You need to kill that fucking ghost.

At my son's words Ben's ghost explodes above me. The red bird cries angrily, turning, away, and the spaces between trees in the light shimmer with the presence of my son Albert.

"Stop it Albert! Don't!"

You don't even realize what he is!

"He's my responsibility!"

My son attacks full bore; I can hear Ben's screams. Once one is subjected to torture it seems to have a way of finding one again . . .

And then the voice in my head. Is it my second self, 2DEE? Or the natives and the Travelers?

BEN'S YOUR WAY IN TO OUR KINDDOM, DEE. COME ON IN . . .

The red fire of Ben's ghost stretches like a spider-

web whose center pulsates and I am sucked through
it—

29

Red Fire

I'm in the sky, or something like it. Red canyons and stalagtites range all about me, below a dark sky. Twenty million shades of red, like flesh, twisted over and under one another.

Its surface is puckered and curved, like glue under a microscope, or the unnumbered meteor impacts of Mars. Goblin Market or Pandemonium. A thousand Babylons. Growing around me.

I want to scream but my body—whatever I am here—feels happy, comfortable, warm.

Each aspect of reality molds about itself, self-similar fantastic, self-revealing, self-correcting, self-agitating, seeking in the edges what worlds now remnants of a former self creep up and in to its fell burrows, like etymology, these are the roots.

Root Kingdom.

Fungal, infinite and varied. The communication system of the worlds and their antecedent, writ larger than any man can see.

"Where are you Ben?"

I'm here.

"I'm sorry for what happened."

You still don't understand what the natives want. Why they brought you here.

"Tell me."

I'd say, you'd better figure it out quick, but I hope you don't.

"Ben?"

I'm alone in the silence. In the middle of this devil's womb.

What do you really want, Dad

I want to endure, son.

You're gonna do that anyway Dad. We're not gonna let you die—

Narrative curved and twisted into my mind. I will redeem myself, and Los Angeles. I will put the Coke bottle onto the counter and receive my nickel. Wooden or platinum.

Something is breaking, son.

It's you, Dad.

◘

I emerge from the Root Kingdom, having never left the jungle, having never left the Root Kingdom. In my life of twenty million ghosts, incombustible enduring ghosts, in some shire without end, what's one more kingdom of them?

What now, son?

You've been gone a week. People might be getting worried.

Shit.

30

Princess

"The natives are still here, John! I saw them outside my window!"

"What?"

"They were right outside my window!"

"What were they doing?"

"Taunting me!"

"Hmm. I'll look into it."

I wonder how many of her ancestral matriarchs were murdered by their husbands … more than one I'd imagine. I go out on the veranda, sipping my drink.

Son?

Yeah?

Can you get me a line through to a Traveler?

Any particular one?

No.

I sit with my blended lychee, colonial master sans natives, spectral transmission line growing in my head…

HELLO DEE

Hi

WE'VE BEEN WAITING FOR YOU

Yeah, well here I am.

WE ARE SORRY FOR YOUR TROUBLES

That's nice of you to say. I'm looking for Sandra. Any idea where she is?

SHE'S ONE OF US NOW. A STORYTELLER LIKE US

You turned her into a goddamned alien?

IF YOU LIKE

I see her, shimmering yellow over the star on the right. My eyes fill with tears. I want to follow her, but she might as well just be weather.

CONSCIOUS WEATHER, JOHN

Fuck that. I want Sandra back.

YOU CAN'T HAVE HER JOHN

Fuck you! Cut the connection, Albert!

WE'RE NOT DONE YET

I'm dancing on the veranda with lychee in my mouth, under an alien sun with aliens in my head, with a wife who acts like an alien. In an alien city on an alien planet. With an AI son who loves me. I could throw myself over the edge.

Don't do it Dad.

I get into the shower and Princess soaps my back, while little spirals of red shimmer behind my eyes.

"Why did you leave Los Angeles?"

"It's been five generations for us, John. I don't re-member."

Her skin is so soft.

125 years then—my Los Angeles is gone. Maybe I should just become clouds like Sandra. Life would probably be nice as a nebula.

I carry this false Los Angeles around inside. My paranoia, finer than any wine.

31

Traveler

I sleep, and it's Root Kingdom. The pulsating red-orange spires and mountains tower aroud me. I take a deep breath.

WE WANT YOU TO MEET SANDRA

On with it then.

YOU MAY NOT LIKE IT

I don't like it already.

"I'm here John."

Why did you ever leave.

"I couldn't take Los Angeles any more John."

I rip through clouds like a supersonic fighter, in dimensions numberless to man, my sardonic river ran, infecting me with sanity—

"I just didn't want to do it any more. All the in-fighting and courtly politics. Worse than the Elizabe-than court was our LA, John, you know that."

I know that.

"When the Travelers came I signed up the second day."

What happened the first day?

"I went looking for you."

Wasn't I home.

"No. And your phone was off. It's okay, John. It wouldn't have changed anything anyway."

I could have changed something.

"It doesn't matter now, John. I'm happier here."

No you're not.

"What do you want to know, John?"

How to die.

32

Natives

I've managed to entice the ghostly remainder of Ben into a bottle—maybe I can impress someone with my ornery genie or something. The man I call Stug is back, hanging around outside my bedroom window, down below our parapet.

I go down and wave the guards away and take a good look at him.

"Having fun with that whore of a wife?" he says.

"Hello to you too."

"Our Traveler friends tell us you had an interesting visit."

"I've had quite enough of interesting visits, but I seem to be cursed with them. Why don't you come in. There's no reason my manners can't be better than yours."

"Funny, a genocidal emperor speaking of manners."

He squints at me as he passes into our small hall. His dark red skin matches their evening sun. He fingers one of our tapestries.

"You know this battle depicts what was actually the mass rape of a village near here?"

I glance at the tapestry, never having taken much interest in it. It appears to depict a glorious battle between humans, aliens, and their machines.

"Terrible as it is, politically correct tapestries are not on the top of my list of priorities, Stug."

I pour us both ice water and sit on my stool. He remains standing but we're both at eye level now.

"That place you visited; it's where we live most of the time. The Travelers too. You could decide to join us, Dee. We would spare many of your kind if you did."

His eyes glint with gold. They fill me with sadness. Why hasn't war made me calloused to the violence of the world?

"What is that place?"

"We order the directions there; and they order us. A control center, if you like. A womb."

"It certainly looked a womb."

"There are things we could show you there, Dee, if you became one of us. Beautiful things."

"I'm afraid my allegiances are complex enough already. Why not return with us to Los Angeles? There are many aliens there already; you would be welcome."

"This is our home. And if you do not leave it, we will kill you. But there is something else I wanted to tell you. Whether you join or us or not, your presence here has attracted unusual interest here, Dee. Forces we can't completely understand. In a way, I'm warning you. Even if you do not die by my hand, there are others on their way."

I reach for Stug's shoulder. His skin is so hot.

"Wait as long as you can, Stug. I want to leave with my people. Give me time, and I'll give you what you want."

"You may already be dead," Stug said.

"It wouldn't be the first time."

◘

He stepped out of our hall and vanished between the stonework in moments. It was the last time I saw him. Even now, after all this time, there are moments when I regret I didn't go with him.

◻

Son?

Dad

What is Sandra now?

She's like me, Dad. A ghost.

But she has a body, Albert. Somewhere.

So do I Dad. So do you.

◻

I know the universe is a living beast, and I bacterium within its horrendous body do not know the sea it swims in. Still, I dream. And in good dreams, those I love are with me.

33

Princess

It would be a pleasurable thing to kill the princess—but I am realist enough to know this for an idle fancy. That she must be eliminated is now perfectly clear to me—and equally clear is that I may not kill her.

"Did you give that monster the bait?" she says, her hungry eyes boring into mine.

"Yes. Stug and his tribe will come to the plaza tomorrow, to participate in a ceremomy of truce, to underline the one we performed in the jungle."

"Our jungle, John. Can I give the order to fire?" She smiles.

I manage to stretch my lips over teeth in something like a grin.

"Of course, princess." I plant a cool kiss on her lips. "Now I must prepare the guards and their weapons. It's possible Stug still plans some deceit; we must be ready for it."

"I'll be waiting for you, lover."

◻

To effect my plan I will need more than human assistance. After leaving the princess I go down to the basement and seal myself in the interrogation room. I strap myself into the chair, the same one where they held me when I first arrived. I attach the electrodes to my head.

I can only hope that I return.

34

Like Dreams

I slip into the princess' mind like into a noxious sea, my boat only barely adequate to the task of staying afloat.

I'm rowing—row row row your boat, into the princess's mind, where nothing is quite what it seems, where even Coleridge fears to tread—

Row, row row my boat, into her castle …

Through the moat into the watery basement where I tie my vessel, shaking out my waterlogged boots in the stinking mud. Mud Man greets me and I shake his hand—he knows what is coming. Servants always know when to jump like rats, from the ship.

Inside a dream, I am inside her—

All the lamplight in the world could not make her beautiful here, where everything she is is plain, rocked forward as in an earthquake, her visage cut into the stone, a massive face seven miles long, over the sky, over the darkening lift of the castle, stone and her eyes.

Mud Man's eyes gleam, and we set to work. Cutting into her huge face, carving out a space to put my commands.

Write, boy, and save yourself from your enemies. Into the chest put your meteorite and herein inscribe its name, to endure forever:

I write on her huge gleaming face, only now becoming aware of my betrayal:

I AM DEE.

Sometimes I still remember Elizabeth's face.

Elizabeth, from Eli + Shivah, the Hebrew god plus the Hindu, in turn named for Seven. She bound herself by the sacred number seven and I still run in her rivers in my dreams. I carve into the bitch's face.

If I were more a man I would just slit her throat in our bed, but that would create some unpleasant complications . . .

If one genocidal monster kills another, is the first redeemed?

The sounds of my hammer in the dark and infinite spaces extend long into my night.

◻

I awake inside the dream; having fallen asleep there. Mud Man is grinning at me. Part of her face has started to move, her eye turning to look at us.

35

Morning

When I awake I can smell breakfast. Downstairs, the princess watches me as I sit down to table.

"Good morning, honey," I say.

She smiles.

Somewhere in her eyes I can still see that grey vista, cold and absolute.

I eat my breakfast and kiss her on the cheek. I hope the seed I planted does its work.

The Mud Man whispered something to me before I awoke—what was it?

I can see his dark eyes, and his lips moving, but I can't hear the words.

Outside, Stug has gathered his army in their regalia, curling leaves and animal horns, emerging from red and violet flowers. With a flourish, Stug turns and presents his arms and so do his men.

Behind me, the princess is smiling; I can feel it through my skin. She puts her hand on my shoulder.

"Are the guns loaded?" she whispers.

"Yes."

There is poetry in violence, as in sex. Their union stirs the gods to action—and me.

With a roar, Stug takes out his daggers and leaps on my Angelenos, opening their veins, and the spider I had planted inside the princess's skull comes to life, its legs emerging from her neck, eating her brain.

I take out my gun and turn it on my city dwellers—now they are not mine anymore.

I fire my weapon. Stug's eyes are like mine.

I open my genie and let out Ben—his red fire lights the galleries and parapets while I scream.

It is true that I am cursed, but I come from a cursed city, and our words are stuffing in a turkey made for you.

Behind me the spiderheaded woman climbs onto my back and I run into the jungle with Stug, cries of horror behind us.

◻

Spider woman on my back inside the world of the trees, with my natives all about me. We swing between branches using her spidery arms, and the natives with Stug in the lead proceed rapidly on their own thin ladders.

Who am I now?

You're my Dad.

Even that is only an act of the imagination.

That's all I am, Dad.

Well then we'll see where it gets us, eh son?

36

Jungle People

Light here is a conscious being, their god or mine I do not know. I sit on their rock and watch its wave-lenghs course over my body. Not revelation or even meditation but a kind of slow construction work: excavating caves in the Root Kingdom.

After a time I open my eyes and Stug is holding his bowl before my lips, a smile on his lips.

I drink.

Be careful Dad.

The Spider Woman twitches over my back. She is excited.

I drink again and the jungle comes alive.

I am a house moving over soil under trees these suns burning my heart. I am a house moving—in more than one direction, shifting, my rooms, and my floors, leaking and learning, dwelling by the road.

Dwell by the road with me Albert.

Yeah I'm here Dad.

We're kings, son.

Sure.

We're animals.

Well, you are, anyway.

We're defiant!

What are you defying?

Everything, son.

Maybe that's the problem.

"Dee!"

The girl Papaya runs me down and we flee into the dusk, with Spider Woman on my back. We sit by the lake and we watch Spider Woman spin her web, her red eyes gleaming.

Don't let me leave here, Albert.

You can do whatever you want, Dad. You do anyway.

I reach into the lake; the water in my hand soothes my heart.

"You saved me, Papaya. You healed me." She smiles.

But no wanderer is safe from wandering. These things I bring with me—all my ghosts—and growing now—they won't let me go. Or rather they insist I go, always.

Giordano Bruno's house—though mine will not be

of memory since mine is so damaged—will be a good model for me. These places I have been, and will still go, shall be rooms in the house I am, carried with me, as long as I live, housing my guests, watering and entertaining them, as we walk over the fjords and rivers of the world.

"They're making dinner," Payapa says.

◻

Some men know who they want to become; others surrender to circumstances. I don't know which is the stronger way to be, but I know I am the latter.

"Come look at the tree, Dee," Stug says, and I come with him, licking my lips.

"Isn't it beautiful?" He smiles.

I nod and smile. "Yes." But I'm not really looking at it. There's something about its curvature I don't like; as though it's looking at me.

"It's your tree, Dee. It will take you where you want to go."

"Oh."

"You've been a good man to us, Dee. We're grateful

to you. If you go, I wish you well. If you stay also."

He leaves me with the tree. It soars above its nearest neighbors by a good forty feet. Its trunk twists like a dancer before rising straight as a shot into the sky. It sways gently. I stand close to it, listening.

So much of the human mind is composed of tree metaphors—we can hardly think without them. We will be tree creatures for some time to come, even though we came out of their branches several million years ago.

Stug understands this as "my" tree in the sense that the tree and I are connected. His people do not use possessive adjectives in the sense of property—rather, it indicates shared fate.

I begin to climb it, watching the sky above. It seems to twist as I go higher, marking my progress from branch to branch.

At the end of one branch I can see Texas, glimmering in Galveston heat. On another is the bus over the LA county border, dark and quiet. A third shows Albert, when he still had his Orpheus head.

The bark feels right next to my skin, and I take my time as I ascend, feeling the tree move with me.

There is some secret the tree is trying to tell me but I am too stupid to know what it is. Up above the treeline the universe seems infinite but I don't see the way down, or the way forward, or the way to reconcile these competing realities, all mixed together in my head.

But at the moment that doesn't seem so bad—the tree could forgive me anything—and I rest against it to watch the sun go down.

Why should reality be as complex as it is? And what does it serve us to tinker so with our own perceptions to the point that our understanding—always insufficient anyway—must scamper and scrape to try and hang on as the world shifts about us? Why did I never make peace with some quiet glade and live there until I died.

Now the sun has set. As my eyes adjust I see Stug and the girl Papaya down below, moving between the trees. Next to me on the branch is the Spider Woman. Behind her spider face I see the princess's eyes.

Slowly I crawl down the trunk, to follow Stug and the girl.

◘

Stug and Papaya flit through the moonlight and I follow with Spider Woman whispering on my shoulder. They stop at a clearing and look back; I duck behind a tree. Papaya whispers something to Stug and then I see the demon rise out of the field, his head misshapen, his huge dark eyes filled with sadness. He is about eight feet tall, and stooped, like an old man, naked, his penis small and wrinkled, the skin over his entire body pale and mottled.

He does a slow dance in the meadow, his arms swaying like leaves. Papaya cries out to him in a pained voice but he does not answer her or change his dance; the demon, if that is what he is, moves just as slow as before. His hands press the earth, his eyes search the moon above us with his eyes.

The Spider Woman is whispering horrible things into my ear but I ignore her; she is still jealous of me and my independence from her.

Stug offers bread to the demon and it moves slowly towards the loaf, taking it with its pale hands, and biting into it with black teeth.

"Are you alone?" says Papaya in a small, sad voice. I

can barely hear her.

"Yes," the thing says. Its voice seems to come from all of the land at once.

"What can we do for you?" she says.

The thing continues to chew. Stug says something then—I can't make it out—and the thing stops chewing. It drops the loaf. It looks at the two of them—as though in astonishment—and then turns and makes its way back out into the night meadow.

Papaya cries out and runs after it, tugging on its huge, spindly arm, but it is not swayed, stepping slowly through the grass. Then Stug turns and sees me, and I know he knew I was there all along. His eyes are filled with an almost religious need, urgent, but he turns away and heads back towards the village.

"Don't go!" Papaya calls after the being. But it is sinking back into the earth, its huge eyes slowly receding behind pale eyelids.

I go into the meadow.

"See, she worships you!" whispers the Spider Woman in her hateful voice, rustling on my shoulder.

Papaya runs to me and grabs my hand. "The god is dying!"

"Gods are always doing that Papaya. You'll die too someday. But it appreciates your offerings."

"It can't die! We will die with it!"

"No you won't," I say, and I lead her back, following Stug in the distance.

"You're going to leave, aren't you," Papaya says. "You're going to leave me."

□

By the fire, Stug tells me: "We were fire at the beginning, and we circled round the sun in gouts of flame. That was before the other sun came, making its strange music, caught in our web.

"We remember you too, Dee, from that time. You were a face of darkness by our moon, shortly after we came to this world. Some of my people revered you, before we had learned to hunt. Before we were men. Perhaps I revered you too; I do not know.

"Do you remember this?"

I shake my head.

"You spoke to us about a land behind your face, over the path that was your body. We recognized you

166

as a demon, and as a demon you wanted us to be your food. Don't worry, that was only your nature. And as a demon we brought you gifts, for a time, as we could see you were hungry.

"Are you still hungry, Dee?"

"Yes." I know he isn't talking about our dinner.

"If you are, then you must go back to that place you came from, long ago. In that darkness your voice is waiting for you."

□

I don't sleep that night, hearing Stug's words echo in my head. What is it that lends to our "civilized" minds this seemingly automatic reverence for the beliefs of "tribal" peoples? Early colonists called it ignorance, though I believe even they would have shared this reverence, though they declined to write about it. I believe it is like journeying into the past, and discovering it is another world, different from this one, full of knowledge now lost to us. I can feel Stug's words take hold of me.

□

I take my boat and head south. The light at sunset filters over my boat washing my mind blissfully clear of thought. If trees dream, it must be of something like this: infinite light.

37

South

There are a thousand regrets I have in my life, but the islands are not one of them. The Spider Woman had been quiet for days, sleeping and nibbling flies in my pocket, but she awoke when I sighted land, and squeaked in an excited voice:

"The place!"

We approached the shore of the smaller island and I waded into the warm clear water, leading my small skiff, with Spider Woman on my jacket. As soon as we hit the sand she scuttled onto it and I felt the air grow thick with electricity.

Spider Woman changed back into a woman before my eyes. Now she was nude and she smiled a predatory smile and took off through the dunes, running like a gazelle.

I tied my skiff to a small tree on the beach and walked into the island.

Up ahead lay a small town, of brightly painted houses. Bird feathers were a dominant decoration, and as I stepped onto their main thoroughfare I walked beneath huge, beckoning wings, as of an angel, or dinosaur.

A woman came out of her house and looked at me in surprise.

"Hev ye kamt fur thase loonch?" she said, smiling.

"I am a traveler, lady. May I have water?"

"Awl blazed be thou," she said, and stepped into her kitchen, returning with a carafe. I drank.

"My woman has fled me. She is under a spell. Have you seen a strange woman, with dark eyes?"

She shook her head and gestured me towards the center of her town. Up ahead, several dozen people were assembling in the square. I understood that the woman thought I should participate. I thanked her for the water and walked towards them.

◻

I must go back to Los Angeles.

I'm hated there, and it is my great forture to be so.

◻

The women were climbing into rockets. At first it seemed to me a kind of suicide, as the rockets were barely big enough for the women. But then it occurred to me the early space program on our world crammed astronauts into spaces not much larger. I did not understand the propulsion system: it shot the women and their rockets up into sky almost silently, colored lights refracting from the booster rockets, if that is what they were.

They sang as they strapped each woman in, and it seemed to me our own space explorations might have benefitted from something like this kind of festival atmosphere, wherever it is they are going.

"How will they survive in orbit?" I asked.

The woman gestured with her hands, making tentacle-like movements, and understood they would be going to see the Travelers. Almost I asked to be permitted to climb aboard, but I know my time here is not finished yet. Even if one Angeleno will accompany me home I feel I will have succeeded. Even if it the Princess, for all her foul moods. And I must find her in any case. None of the women claimed to have seen her. I bid them good luck with their launches. One woman kindly gave me a loaf to take on my way.

I don't trust her on this island. Her mind is like a disease—bred from birth for the most awful kind of machinations. I'm sure she is already working her trickery on some hapless village. Or perhaps they are too smart for her on this island. I hope so.

After a day's walking I lay under a tree to rest, watching the stars come out.

Will I ever have a body again, Dad?

Maybe if you don't try to blow up the sun again.

I want to be like you.

And sometimes, son, I want to be like you.

You wouldn't like it.

Why not?

Too many voices.

□

I must have slept; suddenly it was night and I was staring into darkness, surrounded by the smell of wood loam, convinced someone had been watching me.

I stood, inhaling deeply to fight off a spell of dizziness. I peered into the night, paranoia pumping into my veins.

A man, shimmering in blue, stood in the field.

That's me, Dad.

Then he was gone.

◻

My Orpheus is gone. So is my city, my planet, my sanity and my gun. But I keep them all inside my head.

In the morning I walk to the cliff and look south, along the beach. I see her there in the sand, maybe three miles distant.

I need to find out how she seduced me—not my body, but my mind. What was lost when I arrived, that allowed me to become their warlord? Or was it always something I wanted inside?

How did it feel, Dad?

I forget that you knew it too, son. When you flew over Afghanistan.

But I didn't know that was what you had me doing.

It wasn't me, son. You know it wasn't me!

So you say.

I find a path down the escarpment, to the sea.

Have you opened up a channel to the Travelers like I asked, son?

They haven't been in a talking mood.

I walk faster. The princess is wearing a dress—she must have stolen it. It looks good on her. I get within a half mile when she sees me and takes off running.

She has a runner's body—and I am hardly in battle condition. I'll have to close the gap fast. I begin to sprint, feeling my aging body tug back at me. 'Stop and give up' it says. 'This beach is a nice place to sleep.'

I toss my pack off and accelerate. She looks back and shrieks in rage.

Well, Atlanta, what is it to be, eh?

□

We made love under the rocks.

What fire lives in my blood, still? I feel I have led seven lives. If I were a cat, I'd have but two left.

□

"My weapon is returned to me," she whispers.

I don't deny it.

◻

She is beautiful, and knows it. Aphrodite freshly scrubbed from the waves.

Why is it that some of the most beautiful women are the most evil?

"You must return Los Angeles to me."

"Did you know that I worked there?" she says.

"What do you mean?" I run my hand through her hair.

"I'm over three hundred years old."

"You're getting along in years."

"Ha ha ha! But I don't look it, do I? Listen, Dee, you might as well give up your plan of being our rescuer. We don't want to return."

"But I need you."

"So do my people. They need me here. Now, let us deal with the little matter of your revolution, shall we?"

She stood on the sand and held her hand against her neck, as one might do to check one's pulse. She raised her mouth to the sky and uttered some bird-like clicks and a Traveler materialized out of the sky, drifitng down, a great and terrible octopodal blimp.

She smiled her terrible smile and gripped the ten-tacle as it slithered down, then began to climb it as one would a rope.

One dropped to me and I took hold.

38

Travelers

Our word 'travel' was originally the same as our word 'travail,' and meant "toil, labor." Journey, contrarily, meant "a day's work," or "the travel of a day."

Though the Travelers seem calm, I suspect this conceals their own acknowledgment of the great penalties which attend travel. And though it seems they aid us in our interstellar journeys, I know it is being done at great cost. Perhaps we are their hole card in a poker game we cannot imagine.

Inside the Traveler's body ('aboard' the 'ship') I saw the sucker coming for me and tried to duck but it already had me, leeching the life from my brain, and attaching me to its wall, and I sank into that terrible dream-filled sleep again, in my dream Los Angeles—one which never was but which I fear is coming to be—the green lawns searing into my brain:

39

Hollywood

Hollywood stands like a haunted house, now destroyed. The tumbleweeds blow across the tarmac, and a mournful accordian player strikes up a tune. I strike a match on my shoe and light up a smoke, throwing a nickel into the accordian player's hat.

The remains of the house are plain to see: charred embers and splintered wood work, an exposed foundation.

"Where can a man get a drink around here?" I ask the accordian player, who tilts his head left, indicating a dim door with a single guttering lamp lit over it.

I open the door.

Two women who look like actresses long past their prime and a couple of johns meditate over their drinks. They don't even look up at me. I take a seat at the bar and take off my hat.

"They wouldn't even tell us," the man nearest me says. "They wouldn't even tell us what they wanted." I nod as though I understand. Outside, I can hear the winds starting up. I might be stuck in here a while—better get liquored up.

"Whiskey please," I say to the robot, who pours.

"How's business," I ask the robot, who gives me a cold grin.

I drink the whiskey and order another.

"Next one's on me," I tell the man closest me, who nods without pleasure. "What do you know about that haunted house?"

"Hollywood burned down," he says in a thin voice. "Nobody left but us ghosts."

"How'd it burn down?"

"They said it was the aliens. But I think it was the government."

I take my drink and move over to one of the ladies, dressed in a light blue shift that's seen better days.

"How're you?" I manage, distracted by her cold, dark eyes.

"What's it to you?" she says. "Can't a lady drink in peace any more?"

"I need some information," I say. "It'll be worth your while."

"I've heard that before. The last man who told me

that, I married him. Then I shot him point blank between the eyes, when I caught him with one of those off-worlders. You some kind of pervert, hey?"

"No, not me. Can I buy you a drink?"

"Let me buy you a drink. You look like you need one."

We drink in silence, admiring the robot server's dull sheen. Her red lipstick sticks to her glass. She stares at the bottles behind the bar and says:

"Ask yourself why the Travelers would want to empty the city of Los Angeles. Is it the people they want? Or the city, emptied of its people?"

"What would you say?"

"Me, I'm just minding my own business."

I go outside into the wind, despite my better judgment. Within moments my suit is covered in red dust. I squint and tilt down my hat and move into the wind. The accordion player is nowhere to be seen.

What was it about this city that gave birth to such a specific form of darkness? Is that what the Travelers want? And where is my Atlanta, my evil princess? She should be here too.

The wind is getting worse. Through the dust, I see

the subway sign. I duck into the entrance and head down the stairs. Another guttering lamp lights the way. The trains are turned off but the station is open.

I light a cigarette and peer into the gloom.

This isn't my city. But it's like my city. Just like I'm not me, but I'm like I am. Some poor draftsman's approximation of a universe. The nicotine tastes the same, though.

Are you there son?

Where the hell are you now, Dad?

With the princess, inside a Traveler.

You need to get out of there.

I know.

When are you going to stop thinking with your dick?

I'll let you know. Listen: do you know where this ship is headed?

I can barely hear you, let alone track it. Let me try … I'll get back to you.

Like Foo harvested cattle, the Travelers must be harvesting people. With Angelenos their favorite flavor.

I listen to the wind howl and close my eyes to wait

it out, inside the dream of my dead city.

40

Greenery

Los Angeles has lost its green lawns. It's more than the red dust from the storm—the grass has been brown and dry for a while. Heading into Silver Lake to follow up a hunch, I marvel at block after block of brown.

But at the base of Los Feliz Boulevard, there is a house with something green. Green statuettes, arced across the front of a colonnade of a large house, set back from the street. As I approach I see that they are women, and they are alive—or at least, they have eyes, following me.

"Where can a girl get a drink around here?" says the first statue, her voice thick and reedy.

"We're lonely," says the second.

"Come play with us," says the third.

"I'm looking for Hugibert's house, the Church Father," I say.

"Oh, far away from here," says the first statue, making a face.

"Very far," agrees the second.

"We don't like him at all," says the third.

"Shhh!" says the first, putting her finger over her lips and glaring at her sister.

"Why don't you like him?" I ask.

"Who are you?" asks the first statue.

"John Dee."

"A magician!" says the second.

"Oooh, cast us a spell!" says the third.

"I will if you help me," I say. "Can you tell me where the house is?"

"Very far away from here. Up in the hills. In a distant galaxy!"

"This galaxy," the second says.

"A distant galaxy!" says the first.

"Far far away," mutters the second.

"If you want to know where Church Father is, you must have business with him," the first says, smiling primly.

"Yes, I do," I say. "I'm looking for a friend of mine. I thought Hugibert might know where she is."

"Oh he's a fan of the women, that one," says the second.

"Shhhh!" says the third.

"I don't know he'll want to see you," says the second.

"He will when I show him this," I say, taking out the device.

The statue women are silent a moment.

"Look at that," says the first. "Pretty."

"Take that away from here!" says the third.

"He's up the in hills," says the second in a strange voice. "2348 Moreno. Don't tell him I told you."

"Thank you ladies," I say, bowing. I perform an elementary school trick then, twisting my fingers and moving them to appear one of them is severed. I smile.

The ladies boo me off their stage, and I walk past them, up to Moreno Drive.

41

Hugibert

Even in this simulation the hills of Silverlake bring back bad memories—all my evil deeds. All my encounters with bad men. Though whatever chance is, I feel it's taken a back seat to something else since I came to Los Angeles.

The eaves of the houses peer over the narrow wooded street, and though likely they're all deserted I feel watched.

The light is getting darker—not fading, but getting darker. Pools of it collect around the house at the end of Moreno, under its trees.

Hugibert's Church of S. worshipped aliens—likely it is their broadcasts which summoned some of our first Visitors. Will this simulated Los Angeles have the answers I need for the real L.A.? I can't be sure. But the Travelers are running this simulation from human memories—my own and others. Likely there is something here I'll be able to use.

I walk through the gate, watching the shadows

grow into trees, quivering with electricity. I open the door.

Into a house filled with music.

The walls are so well insulated I could hear nothing of it right outside, but once in the sound is huge, from hundreds of hidden speakers. A symphony.

I go up the stairs.

Hugibert is sitting in his chair, eyes closed, listening to the music. He waves his hands through the air.

"Where are your cultists, Hugibert?"

He does not hear. The music swells.

I want to break the nose on his face, for what he did to Sandra. But I put my hand on his shoulder and shake him out of his reverie. His eyes open and the music stops.

"My poem, it's gone," he says, in a sad voice.

"Do you know who I am?"

"Bring me my water," he says.

A carafe sits on the shelf behind him; I pour a glass and give it to him. He seems not to see me. He drinks greedily.

"Ohh. That sounds right. Sounds about right," he says, licking his lips.

"My name is John. John Dee," I say.

"Like Elizabeth's magician. Tricky cat, that one. Wouldn't learn the rules."

"You kidnapped my friend. Sandra. You and your cultists."

"Cultists? Ha ha ha. You must have been reading the papers. We're a government recognized religion. We have rights. Despite everything. Tell me, John, do you believe you're important?"

He leans forward in his chair, and looks at me.

"What I want to know, Hugibert, is what deal you made with the Travelers. You have a relationship with them, yeah?"

"Oh there were so many aliens. But the Travelers, yes, they were good. Eager to please, after their fashion. A little slimy … but useful. Of course people have said the same thing about me. Ha ha. They told us many things. I wrote some of them down."

"What did they tell you?"

"That's a religious secret, John. You have to pay for that!"

He downs the rest of his water, smiling.

"Now," Hugibert says, "I would like to go downstairs. Carry me, will you?"

Despite my better judgment I push his wheelchair to the stars, then lift him up in my arms, to carry him down. I can barely manage the weight, but it's only ten steps.

As I descend, he whispers in my ear:

"We were going to do very bad things to your friend, John. I had such plans. There are so many ways to use a woman, when you're unencumbered with deadlines. I could tell you stories. Would you like to hear one?"

I step carefully down the steps, gritting my teeth.

"Once, when I was a boy, I saw my face in the mirror. I knew then that I was destined for great things. Incredible things. I took something from her, you see, John, something she didn't even know she had. Something miraculous . . ."

I reach the bottom and drop the old man onto his couch. He bounces slightly on its springs, grinning.

"Thanks John! You're a real man about the house! I could use some extra help around here. And you could use some training! What do you say?"

"How about I kill you, instead?"

"No need for that, John. I'm an old man now. No harm to anyone. Your friend is safe now, anyway. You rescued her! And good thing, too. Women love being rescued. It excites them! Now, where was I? Oh, your contract! What say you to: one lesson of mine, for one lesson of yours. Does that sound fair?"

"What do you mean?"

"Well, I mean, I'll teach you something you need to know, for every little something I want to know. Fair is fair!"

"You go first."

Outside, I can feel something listening.

"Language is, of course, the most powerful way to manipulate reality. This is why my church made at its center a remaking of language."

He smiled at me, took out a cigarette case, attached a smoke to a holder, and lit it. "The reason I bring up language is what lies behind it. For the ancients, sound was a control system of the gods. William Burrough's declamation that language is a virus is actually in keeping with the ancient Greeks' attitude towards religious language: that it comes from the gods, to control us, and to teach us wisdom."

"Language is a human invention, Hugibert."

"Not entirely. Those who study it discover that its structures originate elsewhere."

"I know about your cancerous use of language, Hugibert. You wanted your followers to be mindless slaves, and wrote deliberate nonsense to bring that about."

"But nonsense has a long history in religious language, Dee! Consider the koans. In any case, this is not what I wanted to talk about. The Travelers, Dee, worship certain sounds. By incorporating these sounds into my worship, I found that I was able to influence reality in ways I hadn't even dreamed of. Not unlike what you do with your magic, Dee, but much more powerful."

He took a long drag on his cigarette.

"What sounds, old man?"

"I made a recording of one of them."

He took the recorder out of his pocket.

"Don't play it yet. What will it do?"

"Here, take it. My gift to you."

He passed the recorder to me.

"Now teach me, John. I'm hungry."

There was a knock at the door, and a huge robot with flaming green eyes stuck its head into the room.

"Oh that's Magellan," said Hugibert.

"Jesus."

"Jesus is fictitious, Dee. Magellan is quite real. Don't worry he won't hurt you. Later, Magellan!" The old man clapped his hands. The robot made something like a smile with its face and withdrew, closing the door.

"Language is a vise, you see Dee. Early on, you can make all kinds of decisions. You have all kinds of freedom. But each word you use, each decision you make, binds you more tightly, making you, ultimately, its prisoner. 'Religion' means 'tied again,' you know. Words are what enslave us. You're smiling, Dee. You have a lesson for me now, do you?"

"Yes," I said, and I proceeded to beat him within an inch of his life.

42

Magellan

Magellan, from the Celtic 'Magal': 'scythe.' Magellan's shining green eyes cut through the darkness, illuminating the city as we made our way south on foot, out of the hills.

In his deep voice, he said: "Although you have only harmed my master in a kind of dream, he will find out, and punish you."

"Not if I punish him first, robo."

"He he he."

The Princess has had too much time to get up to no good; I feel certain the Travelers allow her more leeway than they do me. I need to wake up from this particular dream.

Over the empty city we could see the Northern Lights, shimmering in green and blue.

"Magellan, can you accompany me to where I'm going?"

"Yes. If you ask the Travelers to make a copy of me. But you'll need to deactivate this copy first, or it's likely I may get caught in some nested loops."

"How do I do that?"

"I'll show you, Dee."

That thing like a smile lit up his face again as we flagged down a robocab on Silver Lake Boulevard.

"Open the top," I told the driver, and Magellan climbed in through the sun roof, positioning his head carefully through it. I got in the front. "Downtown."

It began to rain and the northern lights became more intense, lighting up the road.

"I love LA in the rain," Magellan said.

The Night Yoga building was still open, and it appeared to be quite similar to the one I knew in the real Los Angeles—gold lettering over its black awning.

I paid the driver and Magellan and I rented mats from the vending machine and joined the class in progress.

Magellan dimmed his eyes so as not to be a distraction.

The night people of Los Angeles looked at us as we came in and made room, and I knelt into child's pose, dreaming of the life I might have led if I had not come to this city.

Slowly I became aware of the Traveler's suckers on my flesh. And I awoke.

43

Interspace

Transitions don't get easier, exactly, but one gains more tools to deal with them.

Dad, you're back!

Do you know where I am?

You seem to be headed for Betelgeuse. Not far from where Foo took you ten years ago.

I rip the suckers off my face, their tiny teeth smarting. I perform my ablutions from the water in the bowl by my creche.

Son?

Yeah.

I want to synthesize that recording I found. That Hugibert gave me.

Give me a moment.

I look around my "room," a kind of organ within the living ship of the Traveler. As my eyes adjust to the dimness I see a kind of laundry-sink-looking object in the corner.

That should do it if you give it the right enzymes.

You see that placental looking nubbin above your head?

Hmm. Yes.

Rip it right out of there.

I do, and it gurgles horridly.

Now squeeze the juice out of it, liberally around that replicator. The wash basin looking thing.

I do, dripping the foul-smelling enzymes over the pit in the corner of the room.

Now just grip it tightly and concentrate. Visualize in your mind what you want it to make.

I press my hands into the lukewarm flesh, holding the image of the recorder in my mind. The replicator organ hums and moans, and after a moment, extrudes the beginning of a small, metallic recorder. I take a deep breath and pretend I'm meditating, waiting for the unpleasant birthing process to end.

When it's finished, I wipe the ectoplasm off the thing and rinse my hands in the bowl.

Play it Dad.

I press the button.

Colored images infect my vision, of worlds I have never seen—spinning galaxies, faces of a hundred different races. I feel water under my feet. The memories of the ship are entering my mind. Like I just blew a huge interdimensional dog whistle.

You just showed up big on my radar in about a thousand different frequencies, Dad.

Over my face, a mask of flesh. Behind my eyes, music. Faces continue to tumble about me, the memory of this species, Travelers avaunt in space ...

Dark cloaks over my face. Over my head, the sky, one I have never seen. I will return Los Angeles to itself.

WELCOME DEE.

Lightning over my shoulders, before my eyes the heath. Purple diaphanous shades marbled and sad cover the landscape, in my inner eye, darklight. In my inner ear, music. What music is this?

HAS IT BEEN SO LONG, DEE?

Are you reading this, son?

Like I said, Dad, you're frickin' huge right now.

I step into the heath. Before, I was not aware of my body when I went away into the Travelers' sleeps but this is different. The two are being merged ... and I am not even physically connected to their fleshy pseudopods.

WHAT IS FLESH ANYWAY, DEE, BUT A
FORM OF INFORMATION EXCHANGE?

Inside the logic of the heath is some logic of my
dark heart.

44

Heath

As one would descend into machine language on a mainframe, or cut into the brain on a patient, I came into the heath. Into the purple grass.

All flesh is grass; mine is purple.

The witch is stirring her pot at the sunset, making her brew.

My face wet with the dew. The continent of stars. The witch sees me, with her solemn face. But I feel she is smiling inside.

◻

I approach her cauldron.

In Scotland, the River Dee bore the name of a goddess. Perhaps my namesake was named for her. In some heath without a name.

Outside my body, the sky shimmers with rain. The old woman smiles. The pot is nearly ready.

Are the Travelers telling me they're like me? That

they should choose these images. That the people of Los Angeles represent for them some vital need.

"Make it short, I've things to do," the witch said, offering me the broth.

I drank it and she came with me, young now, in her witch hat, travelers now bound west to the sea.

◻

The rain pelts down on us and I follow the witch into the dark. I can't see anything through the rain, just dark land and sky, with an occasional tor nudged up against the near horizon.

The broth works in me, summoning memories.

Why did I come to Los Angeles? Who drew me here, and who was I before I came?

"It's coming," the witch says, and I duck beneath her hat.

I lean with her, through the rain, over the purple-black heather.

She is smiling; she has silver teeth.

We move for hours, her body cutting through weather like a trout upstream.

Suddenly we are at a cottage. She opens the door.

"Come in."

She gives me cheese and we eat it in silence. Then I lie down and close my eyes.

Somewhere, distantly now, I'm aware of myself being interrogated on the Traveler's ship. But that is far away.

Then it's dawn on the heath. Pink and red skies peek over the dark heather.

"We can rest if you like," the witch says.

"No, let's go," I say, and I follow her into the dawn, travelers in some world I have never seen but I remember, as one remembers a mother's face from infancy, hovering over, her eyes small moons, orbiting an unknowable Jupiter.

Pink rocks edge their noses above the heath, like islands. We walk between them, west, the sun rising behind us.

Now, when I sleep, I try to remember who I was before I shut my eyes, so that I will be prepared for the man I will be when I awake.

She takes off her witch's hat and her grey-blonde hair is beautiful in the light. She puts it in a ponytail to keep it out of her eyes. Her silver mouth matches the tips of the heather.

"Will I be staying long?" I ask her.

"Not long. Tomorrow, the sea."

This heath is a language of me.

Against the blue sky are black birds, like narrow missiles, shooting over us. We come to the shelter of a tree, and rest under its rustling umbrella. Then we keep moving, into the heat of the day.

She drinks water from a stream, smiling again, with a strange twinkle in her eye.

When the sun is sinking ahead of us we approach a cliff, and below we can see the sea. As black as the heather. Like Homer wrote, wine dark. The wine of the water against the wine of the land.

Why am I made of dark things?

45

The Sea

"We make you a boat," she says.

It takes us a long time. She gives orders with a hand-rolled cigarette in her mouth. The local trees are tough and slow work with my hand axe. She helps me spin rope from purple hemp.

I'm aging in that dark light. Becoming more myself.

Falling into myself. The sail is up on the boat: my cloak. We push her into the water and I climb in.

West.

She has given me a locket, for luck. It has no picture in it, just sand from the beach.

Purple and eglantine clouds hover over the blue black sea. Inside I'm cold. Albert is on radio silence; it's just me and the weather.

If I die here, will I die on the Traveler too?

The susurrus of the sail relaxes my heavy mind.

I remember now: this world of heath and sea is my message to the Travelers. Or at least in part. All I need do is visualize it.

I close my eyes and imagine the Travelers taking my people from their homes, wrapping their bodies in tentacles, and taking them into their wombs, for home.

Though home is a place they have never seen.

Over the sea in the distance, pillars grow, like oil derricks squirted from the wine-dark water, up into the clouds. It begins to rain.

The sea begins to tilt.

The pillars are speaking like birds, kelp sounds, shimmering in the white light.

I put the witch's sand grains on my tongue. They taste of the sea.

The sun sets and I am in a starless darkness, with only the sound of the water. I stand by my mast with my cloak wrapped around me, staring into nothing.

I must find Hugibert on Earth—the real one.

Inside the silence I am resting, like a child in the womb.

46

Return to Earth

I walk through the streets of Koreatown to my address, marveling at seeing bodies on the street again. I go down the hatch to my sewer lair, but there is no sign of Semira. I did not expect there to be.

Inside my apartment, not occupied now for years, construction has started again on the shopping mall across the street. The Los Angeles heat is the same as I remember it.

I pick up the phone and call Meritzia.

"John, is that you?" she says.

"Meritzia, by now I thought you'd have left Earth like the backwater it is. Where are you staying these days?"

"Oh you know me, John, always on the move. You're back in LA. You were in all the papers! Such adventures you've been having."

"I'm surprised people still read papers!"

"Well they're private papers John."

"Are you free for a drink?"

"Where did you have in mind?"

"The Citadel."

"Are we to dress in period costumes too? Ha ha ha."

"Wear whatever you like. Tonight at 8?"

"Don't be upset if I'm a little late, hmm?"

47

The Citadel

I lean against the stonework with a cigarette in my mouth I can't bring myself to smoke. The masquerade of this place is perfect: a pseudo-medieval castle populated with people in a dozen different period costumes. Some android, some human, and now many aliens (though not the Travelers), who apparently grew quite fond of it in our absence, occupying the ceremonial staff positions, of guards, croupiers and cocktail waitresses. Just now one of the guards is eyeing me carefully from his recessed arch in the wall. He winks at me with his green eye. My mouth twitches in return and I take the cigarette out of my mouth.

Observing people has never been harder for me than in Los Angeles, a city that reflects back at you whatever you throw at it, whatever move you make, whatever thought you think. The ultimate instantiation of the Heisenberg principle at work: the people of Los Angeles can't be observed without drastically altering the system. It is the amateur gumshoe who tries to lowball it in LA, trying for low-key moves with fedoras and alleyway shenanigans. The professional lets all his quarries know they're being watched: in LA, it's a compliment.

She's wearing red, of course, to distract me. Dancing with a bunch of skinny robots, programmed to some kind of crack-fueled version of the macarena. She's doing her own thing, whatever it is, no discernible dance steps. She sees me, I'm sure, but lets me pretend I'm watching unobserved.

One of the aliens busts out his sitar and fills the medieval hall with an unearthly wailing—the lament of an alien Orpheus. Though the only wild animals being summoned are androids. He strums faster and the androids kick into gear, doing a kind of ballet, with some Russian flips and human pyramids thrown in for good measure. Meritzia keeps going with her low-key shuffle, waving her arms like a Charleston girl.

I walk over and join her, tilting my imaginary hat, dancing between increasingly frantic robots under the sitar groove.

How many times have I done this: return to Los Angeles to find it unchanged, with only me older, embedded like a hand-hold for a climber in the edifice of Southern California, more absurd with every passing of a year. Here at least I know who I am—or can pretend so.

"What did you do in LA while I was gone?" I say into her ear.

She smiles and dances away from me and the androids are embracing the sitar player, vibrating his limbs like a gang of violent masseurs, and his vibrates the strings to make Stephen Hawking proud, the ten dimensions shook into vital being by an artificial intelligence with a killer rhythm.

I join them.

▢

I wish I could say, things got easier after that. I had saved the city of Los Angeles from itself, after all. I had endured terrible confusions, and committed grave and terrible sins, in order to rescue the people of the city I loved.

But no good deed goes unpunished.

Part 3

Returning

48

I didn't get any answers out of Meritzia at the dance that night, and I never did really get any answers out of her. Though I saw her do a lot of things I still don't quite understand, some of which I think she came to regret.

As to my own regrets, they came when I saw Semira.

She was barely hanging on: the heroin had got to her in a way it hadn't before, and she was a sort of flesh-eaten bag now, containing a tainted spirit. All the ghosts I've lured into my heart and been haunted by and still she was worse somehow. Less ethereal, more fleshy.

I gave her a phone number and a hundred bucks and told her to get help. It wasn't the right thing to do. The right thing to do would have been to shoot her between the eyes, or take her back no questions asked and nurse her as I had before. We had had a kind of unspoken, loveless marriage which was nevertheless full of affection and kindness. And her black eyes so often mirrored my own.

The call came while I was watching the sun go down from my window on Koreatown. It was Jake Smiley.

"I want to talk to you. Got a business proposition."

You'd think, being the savior of Los Angeles would give you some street cred, make it so you don't have to swallow shit for a living any more. But like the joker said, Russia has to swallow twice as many buckets of shit every day as a America, but oftentimes the deliveries are late, or the buckets don't arrive. I suppose I should be grateful the men who still run this town haven't come up with something worse in mind.

The city at night is as frightening as ever. Only now there are more alien voices added to the mix. The long, soft street, and the delight in the lights of the night, the bodegas and the smells and the endless traffic, traffic forever, by God.

It takes me three hours to get to the west side, the subways broke down for repairs and the night roiling to a low, relaxed boil, violence inseparable from humanity, its bread and butter, its redemption.

I knock on the door and they let me in, point me to the boss in his chair.

"I'll have a vodka tonic," I tell Jake.

"We're not drinking today, but we'll pour one for you anyway. Sam, get the man a drink."

"It's not like I need it. Just helps take the edge off."

Sam puts the drink in my hand and I sip it. It tastes delicious.

"Why should I care you went halfway around the galaxy. Why should I care if you went to Egypt, or to Mars? It's got nothing to do with me, nothing to do with my business. We take all kinds of foreigners in this town, and aliens are no different, just a new business opportunity. My family was made on opportunities like this. But what I don't understand is this: yesterday, I go see a friend of mine, get a shipment of some new drugs these little green aliens like, a good chunk of change in it for me, and a good chunk of change in it for my friend. But then, and get this, Dee: my friend tells me as how he's been informed that these particular drugs are to be delivered at a no-profit margin. Now, to make some new customers I understand. The first one's free and all that. But my friend he tells me where they manufacture this stuff, it's on a fuckin' planet that we Earthlings somehow fuckin' colonized with those Squiddie Aliens in the sky, and seeing as how with the what and the what have you, the profits and the losses and the price of eggs on your little pet-project out in Andromeda or wherever, my end of things just showed up short.

"Now you tell me John, what's a guy like me supposed to do? If it were a new operator in town, some new family taking an interest, this a man can understand. That's business. You can negotiate. But this, this sounds to me a little like communism, John. And you know how we feel about communism in Los Angeles."

"I understand that Jake," I say, and take another sip of my drink.

"You do understand. I thought you might. But do you mind me asking, what exactly do you really understand about what I just told you?"

I take another sip of my drink.

"I understand you have a problem, Jake. And you called me over here because I can help you with it."

Short ideas repeated massages the brain, Robert Ashley tells us, and he's right about that. Robert Ashley makes operas for television, and if that isn't the most insane thing ever concocted, then he must be right about that and a lot of other things.

"And I want to help you out with this problem, Jake. Tell me, what would you like me to do to help?"

What follows is a meditative silence in the quiet of the bar. I dare not even sip my drink.

"How about, John, you go and talk to our flippy friends in the sky; you seem to get along with them. Find out just how commie they are. Are they trying to cut into my business? Are they, god forbid, trying to end business as we know it? I'm not asking for my health, John. You know that. And you should know too: I hold you personally responsible for this shit. You wanted to play hero, haul all these sorry asses back to our burgh, you're gonna pay the price. You done with your drink?"

He stands up and plucks my glass out of my hands. "Now get the fuck out of my bar."

◻

Max Planck, the great quantum physicist, opined that science marches forward, one funeral at a time.

And so I began to make plans to kill the little mobster Jake Smiley.

Ever plan to kill a man? It's something most men do all the time. It relaxes you. Makes life worth living. As the great Ben Gazzara in The Killing of a Chinese Bookie once observed: "most men, they get depressed, they start thinking about suicide. Me, I start thinking about murder." While I can't claim immunity to thoughts of suicide, I do find murder more comforting. As DeLillo observed, of cigarettes: "they light a pleasure in the head." Murder does the same. Invites comparisons and revelations, ape-ancestry questions and morbid fascinations with mortality generally, and your own life in particular. Murder, like greed, is good. All things in moderation!

I'm older now and can't undertake a killing with the same aplomb I did as a younger man. More is the shame.

◻

Over the sky the Travelers sail, great sacks of horrendous skin, beautiful in a way. Like strange weather.

Flocks of fat horrendous birds, observers from beyond Pluto come friendly and wrapped in history to our little LA den. Where it stops, nobody knows ...

In part to postpone the unpleasant confrontation I had now decided on, I went looking for Semira, feeling bad for having jettisoned her with a c-note and a bon voyage. Skid row was still near-empty, most of the poor having taken advantage of the significant discounts afforded in rent (courtesy of our new alien overlords) to move into more permanent housing.

A service worker was cleaning up some of the discarded tarps and old sleeping bags former homeless people had left behind.

"Have you seen a young woman? She's a drug addict, black hair, pale, skinny, kind of goth looking?"

"Not many drug addicts left around here, man. You can try down at the health center but they're pretty empty too. I hear most of the druggies hang out on the west side now; you can get condos there now cheap, believe it or not."

"Yeah I heard about that. You haven't seen her?"

"No, I haven't seen your friend. But you want my advice, you should still get out of here before dark.

The people who come around here now ain't homeless, but they're weird."

I thanked him and kept walking, watching the afternoon light reflect off the shattered glass, empty car dealership lots and pale, thirsty trees. One committed rough-sleeper could not be roused; his friend only shook his head when I showed him Semira's picture.

I didn't like to head back to the west side knowing plenty of Jake's men would be around, only too happy to inform him that I was dicking around, wasting their boss's precious time, should they catch sight of me. And my little plan to off the man I wasn't ready to begin either.

I can understand Hamlet a lot better ever since I started killing people: the act never gets easier for me. LA's secrets she holds inside her bones; I can absorb them through osmosis if I play gangster long enough, as I lounge against the whitewashed wall of a Mexican bodega, under the still-lit Bud Light sign. The peace of LA is like nowhere else I know, promising horrible violence in every sweet, longlasting moment. It's a promise LA tries to break as often as possible, I think. It promises death, dismemberment, and horri-

ble bloodshed and revolution, but like God answering
St. Augustine's prayer, not just yet ...

49
The people who come out at night

The freaks come out—everyone knows that—but even by LA standards that night brought me a new appreciation for the term. Right after sunset I started to smell them with my magician radar, blinking over the noosphere. Weirdos coming out to play.

It was weirdos brought me here in the first place. Village of outcasts, heal me, and I will give to you my fealty, over whatever regard of whatever alien sun, though I am not mighty and not as imaginative as some, I am loyal, to your dastardly crooked ways, limned under our dark lights.

They come out in robes, like the Church of S, and I freak out for a second, but then I remember the Church only wears blue, and these are black. Wiccans, maybe. Or Neo-Wiccans.

One takes my hand.

"We've been waiting for you, Dee."

And another says, stepping out of the rubble, "We

wanted to thank you."

It is not ever a surprise to me any more—as Bill Pullman says in Lost Highway, "there ain't no such thing as a bad coincidence," and I think, then, that maybe coincidence is my religion, those things which coincide, and which by virture of their coincidence bind the universe together.

She takes off her robe and the other one hovers behind her.

"We know where Semira is," she whispers into my ear. "Your Sandra too."

"Sandra's dead," I say, not quite believing it.

"No, she isn't," the priestess says, and kisses me. Then a dozen more of them crawl out of the rubble, like rats, and make a circle round us.

So I bound myself again (the meaning, after all, of "religion").

I bound myself to them.

Stars collide and so did my body with her.

One distinctly arrayed energy field.

Sex is difficult in Los Angeles because the democratic character of the city insists we are all equal, and in this equality our joinings take on the character of noble, medieival joinings: they are observed. People gather round. They listen. They know. The gossip of the trees insists your order is a proper order, whatever words you give it are irrelevant, for your body is a word, made to come, and begin, the end, of you.

I am a word of my own too, because I am a magician. Perhaps why these women chose me, though like the Maenads they were hungry too, and not only for men.

After we finish I feel a tension hover round me, and then they cover my sweaty skin with one of their cloaks, and I know it will be difficult for me to speak for some time.

I have returned to my city and its reward is that I should serve even more. Even less of my time shall be my own. And I will know even less of what it is I do.

□

Now it will be me who comes out at night.

They take me to their loft, reciting rhymes, and figures, with the 16mm projectors going at all hours, burning through film like Los Angeles through oil, showing all the dreams and memories of the city. So much is lost to us now. Perhaps that is one of the functions of this cult, though they will not tell me: to preserve and live inside some of these memories, through cinema and sex.

The loft shines with a light all its own. Eager and translucent, under the quilted curtains in their vestibule candle midnight. I drink in that light, remembering who I was, ten years ago, just shortly after I took the name of Elizabeth's court magician. Shortly after I bound myself to empire, all the corners anglophone reciting masses and prayers in our name—no, not our name, but our words—binding us to this inevitable slow destruction of the black hole of Los Angeles now awaking, awaking to the music I am helping to make, squirting gamma rays straight out of the galaxy to regions far beyond our own.

I see in the cult's den 2Dee too. My 2Dee. Doppelganger. Me not-me. Remnant or messenger. Or both. I try to speak but know I shouldn't. Can't even. Words won't do it justice.

I hold hands with the priestesses across from 2Dee and chant. Let me die, I think, let the idea of me die, but it won't. Not yet.

2Dee is smiling.

I know I am not the first Dee. I am becoming the third. 2Dee is older and I am younger. The first is dead. But perhaps we will go to recover his body in Texas.

The upgraded machinery inside me rumbles and clicks then, acknowledging the machine logic of my awareness of the order of my selves, though there is another order too, a spiritual order, and that one is non-hierarchical. One self does not precede another in the higher dimensions.

But then all thought ceases and 2Dee is gone, except for the brief thought that I've passed over, I'm the third now. I've done enough to come this far. I'm keeping my mouth shut, the highest virtue of Los Angeles, and I'm learning, the second highest virtue of LA.

I go to sleep on the pillows and when I awake the cult is gone and I'm naked except for the black cloak they gave me, and I call a cab and promise the robot I'll pay him when we get to my apartment in Koreatown—I still have some old American greenbacks stashed away in my sock drawer.

◻

In the morning I get on the train to Texas like they told me; all thought gone now but to find out who I am. If I am to aid Los Angeles further, and rid myself of some of my enemies, I should at least know this. Too much has happened to ignore it.

I don't trust myself to a plane. I've been known to make computers misbehave when I'm upset.

Three days on a train. The cult women hover behind my vision like flashbulb burns.

◻

I was a boy outside of Houston. I remember the bridge in Harris County, by the library. The smell of sewage. When I smell sewage-flooded waters even now I can remember that bridge, and the children there. The mystery of the sand, the water, and the bridge.

If the pawn learns who it is he serves, does he remain a pawn? Do his moves change? Perhaps increase his chances of becoming a queen?

I close my eyes. When I open them again it's morning. New Mexico. The white dunes all around us. I've been here before too. As a boy, with my mother.

50

The train pulls in to the station in Houston. This cold ball of energy burns slow down inside me. Returning reminds me what I gained by moving to Los Angeles.

I see the faces of the cult women again, in my head.

I rent a car and drive north, to Harris County.

◻

The marshland to the east—its smell—fills me with memories, inchoate, sensible only at a register below thought. Fragments of sound.

I buy a sandwich at a roadside stop and head towards the library. Overhead a UFO is following, shining and silver. The silence over the land is wonderful: like the silence in my head. Cleansing.

What did I become when I left Texas?

The park by the library is about to close. Sunset covers the trees and marsh.

I lock the car and slip through the gate of the park, heading into the boardwalk, over the swamp. The cypress trees are beautiful. Like old women, curled together in the black water.

I see the bridge in the distance.

Just a bridge, over a polluted river.

The same smell.

A little older.

Like me.

I climb down the embankment to the river's edge, watching the red light turn to purple and grey. In the silence, nothing comes to me at all. I am only a lonely man under a lonely abandoned bridge on the edge of civilization.

I close my eyes and the peace that surrounds me is like nothing I've experienced before or since. Just a timeout from the game of life. Soundless and dark.

51

Texas

I awake under the bridge and go to the hall of records for the county, make a donation, and sit down at their computer terminal.

I type in "John Dee," though I know that was not my name at birth. There is only one entry for Harris County. Box 4966A, which I request from the clerk.

John Dee was born in 1941 in Tomball. Died in 1982. Lived at 1648 River Creek Drive.

I get back in my car and drive.

◻

I drive south to Galveston on side roads, watching the city I I knew as a boy.

South to the Gulf.

The sun is magic, and the earth. Men, and women are magic.

I sit on the beach listening to children playing, adults teasing each other, and sketch in my notebook.

I draw Foo, with his large, beautiful eyes.

I see the women's faces again. They want me to get some talisman—theyr'e witches, after all—they want the physical evidence. My robes, or my coins, or my toys, my glass eye, my pencil.

I take out my phone and call a man I know in Washington, DC.

□

For a fee, I run a facial recognition test on myself. Through an unlisted government database, cross-referencing security cameras in the Houston area as far back as data is available, to 1992.

I get one hit: an image—and I see it's me—in downtown Houston, near The Wall of Water—late evening. I'm wearing my cloak.

All day the next day, I ask around the neighborhood where the camera was installed And I find one old woman.

"Jake," she says.

Something inside me rattles.

◻

She takes me into her house and serves me tea. My eyes are wet. Her old face so kind. Memories swim about my head.

"I remember you. You were always poking around then. I thought you were a salesman. But you never asked me to buy anything. Where's your family now?"

"Haven't got one."

"Sure you have. Your daddy loved you. I met him one time."

"You did?"

"Sure. Nice looking man. Kept to himself, like you. He liked to make me laugh."

"Did he live in Houston?"

"New Orleans."

"Do you know where?"

"I think ... I have his card somewhere. You haven't seen him, all this time?"

"No."

"You should visit."

◻

I sleep on the train. I am Jacob Cerrig. Or John Dee.

Inside my head, the women are sleeping. In my mind I lie next to them; I can feel their warmth. Outside, the marsh trees stand dead-looking and proud in the green water.

Aside from the conductor, I am the only one on the train.

My father's name is Henry Cerrig. On his card, it says he's a stonemason.

◻

New Orleans I find so incomprehensible as to be almost peaceful to my eyes. Its transmission signals do not appear to be on a frequency I can easily receive. And if I am anything, I am a radio.

In New Orleans, the radio traffic is a distant, muted buzz. Stories are like antigens, looking for marauders, bacteria and other foreigners. Stories are by nature xenophobic, tied to a tribe, place, or religion. Perhaps that is why my narrative fails me again and again: I do not know where I belong.

The heat is even worse in New Orleans than Houston, and I take my bag over my shoulder in my too-hot dark suit and join a stream of tourists into the French Quarter where I get my beignets and chicory coffee.

Powdered sugar spills over my lapels but I don't care. I climb onto the streetcar and head into the ghetto. Markings much like the old hobo sigils I used in LA alleyways cover the walls here. I climb off at the penultimate stop and go into a bodega to smile and play the detective game. Have you seen this man? No, I'm not a cop. Just a friend. Know who he is? You know who I might ask?

An old Chinese woman keeping her eye on her alien servant sweeping the floor informs me that yes, she cut this man's hair, two years ago. My father's hair.

"What did he look like?"

"Very old. Very old white man."

"Have you seen him?"

"No, no."

I stay in a cheap motel and try not to let the pervasive cigarette smoke convince me to go downstairs and buy a pack. The radio plays jazz and I watch the street. After an hour or so there's a knock at my door.

A man in blue is at the door.

"Hugibert wants to see you," he says, smiling.

Of all the gin joints in all the world … I smile back, trying hard to put a murderous glint in my eye.

"Okay."

◻

Aliens watch from the windows and the doors, torchlight flooding the narrow medieval street. The French knew how to build medieval streets—they were not eager to leave the middle ages. They endure.

Down the stairs. Through another door.

Cultists in blue bow to me and I smile back, throw them a nickel like I'm tipping them, just to piss them off. They let it fall to the floor, spinning.

Hugibert is in a back room, throwing darts. The dart board has a picture of Patrick Stewart attached to it.

"You prefer Captain Kirk, I guess," I say.

The cultist in blue prepares tea in a China pot.

Hugibert says nothing while the tea steeps. Then he steps over and pours it and I see it isn't tea.

"I like my water hot," he says. "In Chinese cups."

"Sure."

"I find it relaxes me."

"You wanted to see me?"

Hugibert steps close to me, his gut huge, protuberant.

"I did, yeah. I heard you're one of these alien-loving types. Some kind of independent operator. Thought I might have a job for you."

"Sorry, I'm on vacation. Sorry to waste your time." I turn to leave and he grabs me by the arm.

"Let go of my arm."

He releases me and smiles. "Won't take you long. It's easy. Just want you to talk to somebody. I've got him right here."

He takes a box out of his pocket and lets out a spirit.

□

It's been many years now; I don't remember. I don't

want to remember either. But maybe I have to. People think—even me sometimes—that you can do something, take a job say, for the money, and ignore what comes with it. Ignore what it does to you. That was Hugibert's mistake. An innocent man, in many ways. A real old-fashioned American. He just wanted a lot of people to like him. But he had to do some really strange shit to make that happen. He's not a very likeable man.

Sometimes I think that I'm the first: Dee Number One. I'm the original and not the copy. I'm the originator. I'm the source. But it doesn't work like that. You don't get to decide.

Sanity this shield I've been forced to do without.

See things, and they change you. And then they want more.

How many magicians over how many centuries made that mistake, figuring: I'm different. These demons aren't real. I'm the real one. I can control them.

But they're just as real as you, man. And there's a lot more of them than there are of us.

I went quiet for a time after Hugibert opened that box. And when I woke up I was in Alaska.

5²

Alaska

Not that I was asleep, you understand. Just a zombie. The mind control kind. Some thing got into my head and shut some systems down and I ran around and did some things for a while.

At least I didn't wake up with blood on my hands.

I woke up in one of the most beautiful places in the world, by the sea and the mountains outside of Juneau.

Juneau, from Juno, Jupiter's wife, the young one. (Though her Greek name, Hera, is related to Hero: protectress). Young Juneau in the wilderness.

Its name in Tlingit is Dzántik'i Héeni: "little flounder creek." All around me the autumn is rushing in. In town the engines annoy my brain—I ask for a coffee shop. The one I'm directed to doubles as a mechanic's work area, so the engine noise is even louder. But they have hot coffee. I sit and watch the men work, unsure quite of who I am.

Are you there son?

How many men before me have woken up in Alaska, too drunk to remember how they got there? Though I'm drunk on something not quite alcoholic. Drunk on spirits ... ha ha ha!

I go outside and ask directions to the library. It should be quiet in there. There is snow coming. I do not have my phone. I do not recognize the clothes I'm wearing. Alaska is the suicide capital of North America.

Inside the library it's calmer; I can almost think. They even let me bring my coffee inside. Calm down, Dee. You're alive. Whatever else may be, you're alive.

◻

Everything I am unfolds. The flaw at the center of Hugibert's thinking is not some madness, but an American thinking. A series of decisions that led us here, to our shared despair.

It is likely many of my adventures have an effort to avoid this central fact. Because I, and all of us, have an obligation to undo these mistakes, and overthrow my forefathers and masters who are watching us now, hoping we stay stupid.

The American Dream—and its ritual purity—invites a champion like me to challenge it. I must dilute its terrible purity and so save my city, my terrible strange city who has drunk from that Kool-Aid and been reduced to myopia and terror.

But first I have to escape Alaska!

I go to work chopping wood and washing dishes with a will and then beg a series of rides south in pickups and lumber trucks through the Yukon, beating the approaching winter in a window of a few days.

Heading south, to my version of Flanders, the fields of Europe's so many wars.

Back to my city. Back to my imminent field, coming round me, energy of slow lightning, of war:

53

Los Angeles

I realize I've begun to limp. Some thing I did to myself in my latest zombie state—whatever it was.

I hold on to the bus stop, outside my Koreatown apartment that I no longer sleep in, though I could. I hold on to the green metal edge of that bench. I am returned, but not even a moment too soon, for the battle lines are drawn, and I am weak . . .

From the bus bench, I draw my power. No less than Samson from his hair and the earth. This is my earth. This is my hair.

Have at thee.

Cry havoc.

□

I see now how wrong I was to imagine that it was a question of distance. Distance no more separates places than do fences keep neighbors apart. They are things of the mind.

And this is truer no more so than in Los Angeles, where every block is its own nation state.

I had imagined, you see, that it was the great distance to Mars, or Alpha Centauri which set about making them foreign but that is not the case. It is only the mind that separates us from them.

But even here I have made the mistake again, you see, of believing: if I can conquer such distances (with the help of the Travelers and their dreaming states) as one can conquer a thought, then I must be the victor of these states of nature. The man in me wants this, of course he does, to have conquered Nature. Even the machine in me wants this, though it knows it is foolishness.

It is the alien part in me who knows the difficulty here truly begins. The magician part in me. The magician in me knows that to conquer a thought is the most difficult battle of all.

Some imagine thoughts as fleeting, inconsequential things. Yes, so too are muons and gamma rays, and the suns they leave behind, equally inconsequential. The size of oceans, continents and galaxies are our thoughts.

The drummer remains a student of the drum as long as he lives. So a magician must with magic.

◻

If I reach into a dream I do it for you, even now. Despite everything, for you. There should not be arbitrary walls between what we need and what we want. In my journeys, I have been bringing them closer. And I will defend myself:

Wolves are coming over the cement. On their backs are women, red bandanas on their heads like foot soldiers for the Bloods, anachronisms no longer, real:

I make them real. They look a bit like Rosie the Riveter.

All of your ghosts, Los Angeles, and all the grave-yards you draw from, in waking and in dreams, I will give them flesh!

I smile into the faces of the wolves and women. They howl, then rush over the hot asphalt, straight at me where I lean like a cripple against the green iron bus bench.

Everything I tell you will be things I have seen, though they may no longer be things that have happened—though they were that at the time. Any student of stories knows they are slippery things. Still, everything I have seen I will record.

They came at me and I was on the rooftop suddenly, above them. Like a boy—an eager Puck—set about my fancies and revolutions as a spinner sets about his yarn. The women howled with their wolves and set about climbing the drainpipes and masonry, women and dogs both.

I summoned the river and it came over Western Avenue flooding many of them, washing them away. I am a river god—or worship one. Dee's ancestors did this. Still four women and three wolves came. Police sirens wailed in some less wet part of the city.

I took to rooftops, jumping, and jumping, my cloak flapping behind me, feeling joy, underneath the palms in the sunset. Behind me, I could hear the wolves. The women were silent, like ghosts.

I am a ghost and a ghost-killer. I serve my city. I serve you too. I promise this, however improbable it may seem.

❒

I cross my arms over my chest, like a medieval solider, and feel the warmth come over me, in the alleyway. Nearby I can hear the wolves, breathing. I feel the silent women, too.

They are the part of Los Angeles I must destroy. Behind them, Hugibert. Behind him, other stories I am still learning.

I am invisible now.

I walk through the alleyways and they do not see me.

I am a ghost.

I am a song without words.

I glide down the midnight street back towards Semira's arms.

I will defeat it. All of it. Though I don't yet know how. Or how much I will lose in so doing. Hopefully not too much. There are still other things I would do.

❒

I come to in the sewer, already standing. How long

have I been awake? Semira is asleep. I can smell she hasn't had her drug. She smells cleaner. My absence has done her good.

Above, I can hear morning in the city. Almost I might be convinced it is a normal morning, or something like it. Where I can go and help at the homeless shelter, and the refugee camp. Where I can eat sandwiches and drink coffee and make telephone calls.

But my phone has been without a battery for some time. And it would not work even if it did have one. None will work for some time, I fear.

I climb the ladder to the street and pull my cowl over my head like a monk and move into the light.

◻

Yes, I was running away when I went to Mars. Seeking enemies abroad when I should have sought them here.

I go looking for my homeless friend, the one I flew with when my jetpack still worked. The movie theater is closed down. No one awake in the neighborhood. Not a sound. Somnolent and terrifying.

I sing a song then, without words, just a white man singing like a Navajo, not knowing the words, only the sounds, but the sounds are close, almost good enough.

Just keeping the ghosts company. While I hunt some of them dead.

◻

Retreat is always an option.

Realign one's energy.

Count one's numbers.

Begin again.

I am parafoiling over the city. Marking my wolves with my eyes.

Marking the women who ride them.

Catching the coils of wind and the thermals to stay afloat. Small motor rolling behind me, under its solar cells.

Before Union Station existed, there was the largest oak in Southern California where Indians had met to settle important agreements for 1,000 years. Destroyed for trains.

Flickering over the surfaces of the running movements of the wolves, I see a house take shape. Donna Reed's house.

Donna Reed's house is like Giordano Bruno's memory house, vivacious and alive, filled with a thousand rooms. All the memory of a race. Of a civilization. Of a man. Who they would burn.

Burn me, I am red.

I am red magician.

I am John Dee. This is my name.

I extend from 1527 to 2015 both forwards and backwards. I am part machine.

I am alive.

Dad?

What is it Albert?

They're coming for you.

Bullets.

I close my eyes.

Duck and cover.

I visualize the approach.

Under the nuclear explosion.

Bullets over my head.

Under my belly the mushroom cloud and nuclear

dust.

Breathe deep.

Sink into the house. Sink into the ceiling of Donna Reed's house.

Outside, nuclear war.

Inside, America.

No nuclear disaster as bright as your sun, within. Eh, son?

Don't start, Dad.

Though you destroy me I exist inside your destruction, a homunculus, virtuous and unafraid, an itty-bitty excrescence outside of your hate and your allies and your wars I exist, inside, a virus, unafraid, whirling like a Sufi dervish into your living room wearing my robes.

"Eh, Donna?"

She is setting the table.

"It's dinner, John."

"Dinner, for me?"

She nods.

Outside, the nuclear daylight is growing. Dust and wind and a thousand things, too great for speech.

"Aren't you hungry, John?"

"Yes."

I sit and put the napkin in my lap.

A lucky man, in a lucky city.

Beset by nuclear war.

Under the spell of an evil magician.

Under suns invisible to Man.

The steak looks delicious.

"Wow, medium rare," I say.

She smiles. Somewhere in her eyes is that feeling of nuclear winter.

"What did you do today?" I ask.

"Today I did the laundry, cleaned the kitchen and took the kids to school!"

"How are the kids? And where are they?"

"How was your day John? Are you feeling okay?"

"I'm not so well actually. I think I should go lie down for a bit."

I excuse myself and go to the settee in the den and lie down. Donna comes over, in her starched and pleated house dress, to stand over me like a guard dog.

"I think we should have a talk, Donna," I say.

"Yes," she says.

"Los Angeles, it's gotten pretty bad. It hasn't been fair to you, fair to any of us. I want to know that you understand that, that you don't blame me."

"Blame you, John? For what?"

"For everything. For everything that's gone wrong."

She says nothing. I sit up on the settee, looking at her.

"I need your help, Donna. Against a very evil man. And against a lot of people who support him, some of them against their will, but some not. Help me."

"This morning I was in a far off room, John, with black walls. They were coming to eat me. The walls, that is. It felt good. I wanted to be eaten."

"It's part of his spell, Donna."

"I don't think so," Donna says. "I think it's me. I'm the spell. Don't you think so, John."

It was then I saw she was holding the kitchen knife.

"No, Donna, I don't think you're a spell, I—"

She stabbed quickly and ferociously, the tip of the knife grazing my side before I seized her arms. She was extraordinarily strong.

"Let go of the knife, Donna."

"I wanted to talk to you," she says. "I wanted to talk to you so bad."

"We'll talk now Donna! Let go!"

She did let go, dropping the knife onto the carpet. She walked to the window as though nothing had happened. I picked up the knife and put it in my robe and went to stand behind her.

The walls began to shimmer a bit, yellow electricity running through them.

"John, I have to tell you something. I haven't been faithful. I mated with a demon in the basement."

Down below us I hear a huge thumping. Someone knocking.

"He told me he would make it better John! That he knew who I was! Who I was before I was with you!"

I'm already running, to the cellar, knife in my hand, spinning down the axis of the stairs, suddenly Escher-esque, collapsing in on themselves as I tumble down them into the black cellar.

It smells of earth—coal, and sweat, and sulfur.

Around me the spider fingers cold as dark water curl over my body and the walls are gone. I stab with my knife but it meets nothing—only empty space. Spider fingers tighten around my neck.

"What did you think I intended when I hired you,

John? Did you think you could just walk away? That I would forget?" It's Hugibert's voice. "No one walks away from me, John. Nobody. I want to teach you a lesson, John. One you deserve."

A terrible squeezing. I cry out.

"Donna!" I shout. There is no reply. Only the hissing of the spider. I see her then, holding a lantern, in a dress from the frontier, white Victorian. In her hand is some kind of iron sigil.

"Donna!"

Behind her is another woman.

Flames enclose us, cold fire. The spider is burning. I can hear it screaming, silently.

"I can destroy you with a word," Hugibert says. "You are only a kind of thing inside of my dream. I hate you! And I know something you don't, John. You and your girlfriend are running out of time. Los Angeles is a kind of machine, did you know that John? It's a machine that makes money. And you know what else it makes, John? Special kinds of weapons, John. I've been promised the right to test them, John! I hope you enjoy it."

Fire all over me, cold and blue and white. The

women are dragging me up the stairs. The sigil is shaped like a 1950s UFO. Like Foo.

□

When I wake up I'm still burning, the cold blue fire all over my body. Donna and the other woman are talking in the kitchen. I look at my hands and watch the flames. The shapes of the plasma are so alive.

"Hey," the woman who isn't Donna says. I look at her. "You feeling all right?" she asks.

"Who are you?"

"I'm Sandra."

I feel faint. "Can't you make this stop?" I ask, looking at my burning hand. "It's driving me crazy."

"We're working on it," she says. "Drink some water." She hands me a glass and I drink. She returns to her discussion with Donna in the kitchen, in hushed tones.

The blue flames licking against the water glass are beautiful, refracted. I close my eyes to give my brain a rest but then I feel even dizzier. I stand up, and wobble for a moment. I place the water glass on the table and walk into the kitchen.

They stop talking when I enter.

Sandra has this strong inner light. I realize she always had it, but now it's almost visible.

"I missed you," I say.

"We don't have much time, John. That thing is still in the basement. Are you okay to walk?"

"Yeah. I can walk."

They put a winter coat on me and they put on coats too, and mittens, and scarves, and we go outside, and it's snow as far as you can see. Strangely beautiful. Northern lights in the sky, scouring the atmosphere. What latitude are we at?

"We have about four miles to go, John, can you make it?"

"Yeah."

We walk into the cold.

◻

I can feel the cold in my boots and the fire over my skin, all around us white on white under green and black starless skies. If only I am true to myself, I can survive anything. Understanding darkness, like a dream, involves leaps of faith and logic, to know the words and logics of beings and worlds nearby but not our own.

Like winter is not our own, not quite, winter is someone else's.

I am white and scarlet inside the white world, the women moving steadily over a land I remember from somewhere in dreams.

If the moor—the heath—were my home, with the old lady and my boat … this is like a neighbor's house, this winter landscape, not mine but still familiar, like the fire over my skin.

Sandra looks back at me.

Whatever my shadow is I can strengthen it, like holding my hands over a flame.

There is a building up ahead, non-Euclidean in shape, diagonal against the white horizon, a black corner of safety.

The women speed up and I follow them, watching the breath out of my mouth. It looms over us like some great ship. Sandra kneels and gives me a boost up to the edge and then I reach my hand down to help the women climb up, into the bowels of the place. Hollow and only slightly warmer than the white landscape outside. Firelight from some distance I can't measure reflects off its walls.

"Where are we?" I ask.

Sandra places her finger over my lips.

Suddenly I remember my cult women; here with me all along, in my head.

I follow Sandra up the stairs into a bright room. Like a Star Chamber—I remember it—or a communications center. We meditate then, together, without speaking. Some soundless being far away is measuring us.

Begin to war against great powers and one needs so many allies—they come in if you let them. Though their agency will be beyond your comprehension.

I inhale the cool air, breathing, letting the place do its work.

Then Sandra kisses me and I remember her. All that we would do together.

Like some seal. Not a promise but a seal as over an envelope. A message into our future. In a language I am not fully literate in.

I'm asleep—or half asleep—in the bed in the room in the fortress. Fortress is not the right word but it's close—a cousin to what it is. The darkness is like a slow, pleasant weight over my forehead. Outside, the women are talking again.

It has occurred to me that I am in the spirit world. Or quantum dimensions in the multiverse, if you like.

But it is also a spell—I know that. Hugibert has captured some corner of it, turned it into something like his. Not his, but something like it. It's stronger than him, of course. More ancient. All this I feel in the air.

Overhead I see a metal shape, like a large metal detector, or manta ray. It hovers over my head, three feet away.

It's scanning me. Donna comes and holds my hand. Colors swirl over my vision. I feel it pinning me to the mat beneath my back, like a strong magnetic field. Donna squeezes my hand tighter. Dimly, in the darkness, I can see Sandra, on the phone. How did Sandra escape that fate she had dealt herself? I have to remember to ask her. I want to ask "what is happening?" but my mouth won't move.

I listen instead to the scanner. Who is behind it? What wavelengths does it reach, spiriting away ghosts of my consciousness to the aether?

I try to sleep. But I feel a humming in my brain. When I open my eyes the women are gone. So is the scanner.

I'm alone in the fortress. The magician's house. The magician's prison. Like Prospero's island.

On the hat rack I find my hat and coat. My galoshes. I'll need those; there's been a plumbing leak; two inches of water are covering all the rooms. It stinks of mildew. Fluorescent lights flicker intermittently in the distance and I go to investigate. Investigate, gumshoe. That's all you're good for. Even if you never figure anything out. At least I can say I turned over a few rocks and watched the bugs. (Perhaps I'm one of them).

There aren't many fluorescents and they light only parts of the corridors. I pick my way between the pools of light.

Rosie the Riveter and Donna Reed. A bunch of wolves and a big spider. Hilarious, in a way. Just hilarious, Dee. I can almost laugh. Instead I listen to my footsteps in this hollow hell. They should tell Nietzsche: having gazed long enough into the abyss, not only will it gaze into thee, but you'll become part of it. You'll set up a whole fucking communication system. You'll build a turnpike and set up toll booths and little burger joints, along the route from you to the abyss, and back. Real friendly like. Maybe the occasional roadside stop with a stone altar for child sacrifices.

There's a moaning up ahead. Echoing. I try to follow it but it's coming from no clear direction. Then I see a face, white against black, in isolation, like a living mask, cut into the wall, its mouth a wide round mime's 'O.' Its eyes look at me. I look back. He seems familiar—if it is a man.

What are you doing, Dee? Just what—

Suddenly the mouth speaks:

"You're saving the world Dee."

I shake my head. The face smiles. A little malicious glee in its expression.

"You know what you need to do Dee. Find the prince. Give him your magic. Tell him you love him."

"Nonsense," I say, and set off again down the hall, with no more idea of where I'm going but eager to put some distance between me and that smile. My footsteps echo down in front of me, like water droplets in a huge, still lake.

I find a patch of wall and lean against it. The cement feels good against my shoulder and gives a little under its pressure, like a thick mattress. I can see down the next hallway—light of some uncertain source. It's a very long hallway.

Perhaps I am inside Hugibert's mind. But I don't think so. It's a real place, just marked by him. Listening to him. Feeding on him, like a demon on Faust . . .

It's so lonely. I start down the next hallway, my fingers trailing along the soft walls. I feel like a drunk, stumbling home, though not to any place a drunk would want to call home. Or anyone else human.

Sing a song, Dee, keep yourself company.

"Oh once I was a tiger, I lived in Old Savannah,

With a trumpet and a bucketfull of gin!

I trapped the mice between my paws,

And set to juggling them!

A yo ho ho!

A yo ho ho . . ."

In the long nights the women keep me company.

Even if only in my mind.

◻

There are stairs now, the color of ash. They're soft, like clay. I start up them, smelling moisture up above. The walls are warm and luminescent about my body. Every tenth step the stairs turn. Go up, Dee. Up, up, and away! Able to leap small bales of hay with a single stumble! John Dee, friend to humanity, genocidal maniac! Wanderer in sewers across the galaxy. Drug addict, chain smoker, no-good bottom-dweller. Womanizer. Beach bum. Human detritus. Ash and ash and ash … spiralling in the wind—

After a time I stop thinking and just climb.

◻

Now there is no ceiling; I have climbed the stair. The clay is like the surface of a distant empty planet with no stars or sun. I still smell water though. Shadows all about me—like friends.

When will you stop, Dee? When will you learn to

be happy with what you have? And what could that possibly mean?

The horizon is black and the clay is grey. I follow my nose towards the water.

There is a lake; I can see it! It's beautiful.

I remove my clothes and slip into its cool embrace.

◻

Sandra is soaping my back in the tub. I lean back against her breasts.

"How did you come back?" I ask.

She says nothing, but opens a bottle of shampoo and lathers my hair.

"That place, the red organic walls—the womb of narrative or whatever—you were in there. Part of that thing. A big crazy ghost far away."

"Mmm," she says.

"The wizard, where is he?"

"Hugibert? He's close. Don't worry. We have him under control, for now."

"We do?"

"Donna is working on him."

"Hmm. Like you're working on me?"

She pours warm water over my head.

"Now you do me," she says.

I do.

◻

I wonder if this is how Albert feels. Floating be-tween worlds. Given some power to effect change in several, without enough information to develop any fuller understanding of the worlds he's in. Working with incomplete information. Cut off from anyone who understands him.

I hear Morse code in the distance. I get out of the tub.

I get out a pad of paper and a pen. I don't know Morse code but I can tell a dit from a dah. I write them down. The message is on repeat. Sandra helps me translate it.

It reads:

YOU ARE NOT ALONE. THIS IS SEVENTEEN, REPORTING. WE ARE FIVE LIGHT YEARS OUT. WE'RE LOOKING FORWARD TO SEEING YOU.

"Who is Seventeen?" I ask.

"Some friends of mine."

"What happened to Sixteen?" I try for a joke.

"Their predecessor. They were killed."

"Sandra, you mind if I ask: where are we?"

"At my house."

"In Los Angeles?"

"No."

"Where then?"

"In between, Dee. Just how you like it, love."

There are books on her shelves. Some of them she's written.

I fall asleep on her bed, trying to forget everything I ever knew.

◻

Returning to the heart of Los Angeles. The heart of America. What dark heart beats below my own, reminding me, of all my mistakes, and all the ones I'm still to make…

Returning to LA's heart, in its den, in its patient horrible den, the core at the fiery center of an ancient evil, the one Burroughs knew was waiting, and waiting, for a magician to harness it...

Bigger than Grendel's mother and bigger than the Dragon is LA's heart, the innocent girl in Catholic schoolgirl uniform with a knife taped to her leg and a mouth like a sailor, black eyes and blacker habits, ready to rip the rug out from under all the people at once...

LA is innocent like a child soldier, and just as deadly.

Hugibert—and the others—they're the recruiters. Telling that little girl: blow off your parents' heads. Follow me into the dark.

Follow me into the dark, and yield to none you find there, until the darkness is your own.

◻

I wake up and Sandra and I make breakfast. It's the happiest I've been in a long time. Then we go upstairs and wake Donna. She doesn't look well—hungover, or worse.

"Do you want to stay here?" Sandra asks.

267

"No, I'm coming."

We go outside of Sandra's door into Los Angeles.

Into Echo Park.

54

Echo Park

LA is so full of spirits you can cut them with a knife. LA is a broadcast center, and Echo Park her little echo chamber, ricocheting that electromagnetic radiation from beyond Pluto around until it all makes a kind of sense.

Years ago I fought Chaimougkos—a big crazy alien—but he wasn't as bad as this homegrown evil. Civil wars are always nastier than foreign ones. Looking into your brother's eyes, or your uncle's, and knowing: now I must kill part of myself.

We go into a café on Sunset, just north of the park.

"First we do one of Hugibert's lieutenants," Sandra says. "Martin Oster."

Inside my head I can hear the dit-dah-dit of Morse—I'm starting to understand it. The ships of Seventeen. They're saying:

WE'RE GETTING CLOSER

◻

We pull up outside the house, the same one I entered years ago to talk to a crazy man. Feels like a previous life. We walk straight up to the front door together. A little security camera stares down at us.

I try the door and it opens right up.

I go inside.

No man is an island and no phenomena occur in vacuum. To seek power is to study the relationships between phenomena: magic as a kind of applied science.

Back in the dark. I feel the women behind me. The door has closed though I did not hear it. I can hear a skittering, like insects, or rats. Scratching on tile. I step forward into the dark, listening.

I shut my eyes, and flip the switch.

Come with me:

(sing a little song)

(don't tell me how long we're gone)

I begin to weave with my fingers, spinning little cables made out of light. Stretching before me and the women, our faces now illuminated by the threads, is a railway stretched over infinity. White-green lines over an endless night.

Above our heads I can see the Church's oligarchs staring down, like malevolent satellites.

Just a little home invasion and intervention.

I spin my fingers and Sandra and Donna make a train with their hands out of the light. They caress and mold its surfaces into a serviceable handcar.

Bearing in.

Bearing in and bearing below.

Following another psychopath into his mind. Into his mouth.

Bearing down. Just a runaway freight down into someone's personal hell.

Lines flash over our heads. I spin the green cables out of my hands. Sandra works the engine, blowing the coal hot with her mouth.

Donna reaches for the whistle cord.

"Not yet," I whisper. She holds her hand over it.

We're accelerating. Hurtling down a terrible hill. Gravity pressing in on our faces and our backs. I weave faster, my hands spastic, curling around.

"Now," I say, and she pulls the cord.

The sound shatters the shapes around us. Even the cables I've woven. We're hurtling in the dark, caught in a well of a dark sun. Curling in, and down.

I can see his face over a black hole, his cruel eyes flickering as he watches us approach. Blue eyelids and curling eyelashes. Black shimmering eyes.

"Hold on!" I shout.

We fly down the last hill and are in his brain. I feel sticky and wet. The women look pained. The air is full of a horrible electricity.

I feel his body move. Martin Oster. He's at a café. His hands resting on the table. Another man is talking to him. They're discussing a killing. No, a pretend killing. A movie. Some fetish thing. Children covered in blood. They discuss the logistics and the numbers. I can feel his lips move, as a heavy weight. The women have stretched their hands over their ears.

I move his hand. I know he has a gun in his pocket.

He knows I'm here.

He's toying with me.

I make him reach for the gun.

He wants to.

He takes it in his hand. I feel its weight.

His lunch companion looks worried. "What's wrong?" I hear him say.

"Bad spirits," he answers, as from under the sea.

"Do it!" Sandra shouts.

I take his hand, and raise the gun up to his head. His companion screams. I squeeze the trigger.

◻

We're outside the house. Me and Sandra and Donna. But there is no house. Only a vacant lot. We hug each other then. Rest next to each other's warmth. But part of me is still down inside the dead man's head. The one who never even existed, now that I made him die.

◻

LA is like Chutes and Ladders, and the chutes lead up, and the ladders down, but there's no devil and no god, just different worlds, stretched between the city as you might remember it and the city as you know it is, fighting and dying inside, a terrible ember burning its truth out of your eyes. Los Angeles is this little board game in your head, that comes out of your hands and makes the world spin around you, reminding you of ten thousand Heisenberg truths in every instant, that the world is your play pen, and it can be any game you feel like playing—any game you think you can survive.

□

Have you ever killed a Church before? We've tried many times. In Gobekli Tepe, 9,000 BCE, we buried it up with bones. Covered it up with dirt and rocks, that dead little underground temple. That was in southeast Turkey. But the locals never forget. And the priests keep remembering, writing the stories down and burying them in pots...

Like some kind of Hindu pattern, the villain with a hundred thousand faces, with his foul angel dust mixed into the night, falling into the mouths of converts like rain into gutters, running down into the network of the city's thirsts.

Killing a Church is like teaching a class. You have

to start where they are. You tell them that everything they knew is wrong. Everything they thought was true is only the faintest scratch on the surface.

The problem is: the only way you can kill a Church is by making another.

Humans need programming; the question is, what kind of code is it gonna be?

The Church of S. will die by my hand, and my friends' hands. But what are we putting in its place? Justice is like weather: it's wind and rain and stars. Far away and close. We're these terrible small gods smote on the earth with only our words, and our memories, guiding us...

Son, are you there?

I'm worried Dad.

Me too.

◻

My name is Dee and I'm a magician. I still don't know what that means. Maybe it means: I'm a man. I've got some friends, and I've got some memories. Some enemies too. I live in this city we built, and we hardly know why. Over us are the stars, far away. I've been to some of them. But I still can't tell you what it means.

◻

I make love to her in her bed, between this world and hers. Between my body and her body. Inside this grief of life.

55

Echo Park

It's raining. Easier to kill in the rain, as though no one will see.

Maybe that's what that boy saw in me: the murder in my eyes.

What would I say to justify my killings now? She would have done worse things, if I had not acted. It was a punishment. I did it for me. And I did it for us. It was necessary. I can tell myself that, and believe it.

Killing cultists is appropriate in Los Angeles, as there are so many, and humanity's religious heritage is composed in large part of centuries-long internecine wars of aggression between priests, extending back at least 10,000 years, probably much further. Two shamans with a grudge. Or three.

I bear a grudge, as is the gumshoe's right. I have a gun, and I know how to use it.

I lead the charge and I give the reasons why: I did it because I wanted to.

◻

Rain confuses Los Angeles. We do things we do not expect, in the rain.

The women and I are rather heavily armed. Always plenty of armaments for the getting in LA, if it's your desire. We've rented a limo: the one kind of vehicle that can idle for an hour in the hills of Los Angeles without attracting notice.

It occurs to me that these killings are not enough, not by a long shot. The spell of one evil magician is hardly the tip of the iceberg. But the women want it. And so do I.

I sit behind the wheel outside Hugibert's house. Donna loads the rocket and Sandra readies our machine gun, to cover us from the roof. I polish my .38.

Ripple through me, and I will through you.

"Load the machine gun, Sandra."

"It's loaded."

I can hear her shouting inside; the limo didn't fool her for long.

Who is an innocent in religious conflicts?

No one is truly harmless.

Still, the issue is academic. We aim to decapiti-
ate the Church's leadership. To liberate Los Angeles.
And to sastisfy my gumshoe's brain, sniffing out more
leads...

I can't tell you about killing Hugibert's wife; not
yet. I want to, but not yet.

I have to tell you more about New Orleans first,
some things that I skipped over.

56

New Orleans

That city had seemed closed to me, New Orleans. Or perhaps there were simply too many doors. I met Sandra there. Before I returned to Los Angeles. She told me part of the story of my life.

It is tempting to believe her.

She has the most beautiful laugh. You know she writes stories? Some of them are about me, she told me.

◻

I suspect now that Sandra didn't want me to meet my father. The inertia, as it were, of my adopted identity demanded that I not be sidetracked. I had become too useful as a gumshoe. Whether she loved me or not. Whether she was lying or not. She knew I would do as she asked.

◻

She took me into the barrio. She stepped over the bed, taking off her shirt. I put my hand into her curly hair, and kissed her. She took me in her hand.

I am only a man. I took her body in my hands. I know she was not the same Sandra I had known, but none of us are ever the same. In some ways I think it was the Sandra Chaimougkos loved. The woman with her eyes on the galaxy.

I have my eyes there too.

Spinning around my hand.

Sandra! I love you! Where are you!

I'M HERE JOHN

You're a liar.

I NEVER LIED TO YOU JOHN

Why did you tell me to do those things.

BECAUSE YOU WOULD DO THEM JOHN

57

We killed her outside her house. Sandra ran the machine gun putting maybe forty bullets in the fat woman's body, skittering her like a sack of red leaves over the fancy porch. Donna blew the front door off and I screamed for them to get back in the car—the limo—and I drove in silence.

Easy to tell, I know. To say, we killed this woman, and she deserved it. And she did. People benefited from her death—thousands of people. But it's not the kind of thing you can prove in court. Or forget, when you want to.

◻

I wish I could tell you, Sandra and I fell in love, and we moved far away from here, and lived happily ever after.

However, Sandra and I did set up house together. A house like Giordano Bruno built: a memory house. One to house all our memories we were making together. In all their colored splendor.

We named that house the house that Jack built. Though it was Sandra's work too. And mine.

But we gave it to Jack, hovering over the sky:

Our new friend, Traveler Jack.

I'm clinging to his tentacles while Sandra perches on his head.

I'M GOING TO TAKE YOU TO MEET SEVENTEEN

For some reason I'm smiling.

◻

The colors fly by us; I'm laughing. The Travelers are men. That is, they are human. From some future I cannot imagine.

Over their cloudscape not made of water but the fluids of their native dimension we are streaming, accelerating towards out goal.

What is the darkness in me that I nourish? Where does it come from?

Why do I need it so?

Lightining over the deep; I'm still laughing. Sandra is screaming too—a sound of both joy and thin madness.

◻

We are at a docking station. The men—the Travelers with their great tentacled arms—are moving around the ship like organic moons around a metal planet. The dock opens and we glide slowly into it. Men in white suits spray the Travelers down with foamy liquid, a kind of food plus lubricant, I learn later.

Still the electric storms outside color the metal of the ship, flashing and fulminating. I am unable to speak.

What is the darkness in me but my soul? And if my soul is dark, what does that mean?

◻

I'm resting now, with music playing from a small screen. In a small visitor's cabin.

"You're awake," Sandra says, coming into the cabin and sitting on my bunk. She's dressed in all white.

"Who is Seventeen?" I ask.

"They're explorers. They've been to the deeps and returned. One of the first to do so, they tell me. Are you all right? We were worried about you before."

"Why?"

"You were screaming."

"I don't remember."

"The Travelers were waiting for us to make those kills, John. When we did, it opened something up. Destroyed some locks that Seventeen had been waiting for."

"What does that mean?"

"It means Earth is going to turn into a transit hub very soon."

"I thought we already were."

"Not like this."

"It's a fabulous ship. I remember arriving."

"Yes, it's enormous! I've been exploring for hours and only seen 10% of it. Come see with me!"

"All right."

The room stretches down and at angles perhaps 3,000 meters, revealing in the huge room men and women sitting and standing in nooks and crannies—

the largest office space I've ever seen. Like stepping down a Greek temple's steps. Where the center would be—where Aeschylus would have stood in his in Athens, is blackness.

All around us human beings smile at us and wave, as they move their hands through waveforms and speak into microphones. But as I go down further with Sandra I realize what kind of a ship it is, and why Jack brought us here. They too are memory devices. That is, their 10,000 strong or more workstations are not things like "engineering" and "communications" and "weapons" but states of being.

States of being human. I hold Sanda's hand and we step into a young woman's work area.

"Hello," she says, speaking through her translation device, "I'm Elizabeth."

"Hello Elizabeth," I say. Sandra kisses me and is gone.

"John you've been away for a long time."

"Yes."

"Let me embrace you."

She holds me in her arms. Redhaired queen. Or something like it.

◌

"We expected you later," she's saying. "Most algoirithms had you at three decades out."

"I see." Although I don't.

"How was your journey?"

"All right."

"Are you feeling disoriented?"

"No more than usual."

She's smiling. She has a beautiful smile. I remember it too. "What do you know, John?"

"I know why I came here."

"You remember!"

"Yes. Show me the coordinates."

She races her hand over the field and I see the Earth, arrayed around our remaining targets. Not to be killed any longer! Though perhaps now I am giving them a fate worse than death.

"They'll survive it?" I ask.

"These nobles of your era were trained to negotiate—and submit—to aliens. They're conduits, John. I'm coming with you and Sandra, to finish all the good work you've been doing. But we don't have to talk about it all now. I'm surprised you remember!"

"I am too. Tell me: what is this ship?"

"We're the returning wave, John. From everything the Earth sent out. Just a Newtonian opposite reaction. Everything the Earth has done. It's coming back."

"That doesn't sound good somehow."

"We'll find out."

◻

They strap me into one of the stations.

Will I still be a gumshoe, after the things I am about to do?

58

Los Angeles

Once I told a woman I would help her. A woman named Los Angeles.

"Come help Los Angeles, John!" With a face like murder over her body.

Into the stone streets I followed her, under a shining blue sun.

"I needed you more than anything!" she shouted. And I couldn't say a thing in return.

It's the Hierodules, I realize that now, the temple slaves who've since fled the Earth—my doing—so many competing masters of narrative…it was them. This is their punishment.

Galactic Seventeen has been very far away. It is not entirely accurate to say that its crew is still human. But then, am I still human? I still appear so. I still feel human. Elizabeth is warm, like a human woman. But she carries things from far away, even as I do. Things we don't have words for.

Often I have reasoned that my stories are betrayals.

Having done the things I've done, as with any killer or spy, my chief task is to keep mum. But I am writing my deeds down. One can say: well, I serve future generations. I betray my bosses to serve humanity. But this argument too is specious: if I had kept mum, none would ever need know of these terrible things. Having written, all the plagues I have encountered will plague you too, and your descendants. So I am damned twice. Once in the doing, and second in the writing.

You can see why priests are always so eager to burn the holy tracts of their competitors: who knows what spirits lay tied up in them, waiting to attack.

□

The ship and its crew, gone far away and now returning, and me too. You can't go home again, but you can still influence it. You can stand in the same spot, and say "I was here."

I was here, goddamn it. I will infect you with this narrative plague if that is what I must do. The story.

YES JOHN

Who is that

IT'S ELIZABETH JOHN

You're here.

WE'RE DOCKING. YOU WERE ALWAYS MY FAVORITE MAGICIAN.

◻

The lights on stage go up. I am in Los Angeles. A terrible town for theater. I have forgotten my lines. The audience is stirring.

"I am John Dee!"

They are listening.

"I bear a message from the Queen!"

The demons, smiling actors in spiky costumes, rush out from back stage. As if I were Faust. They howl and scream, pretending to tear my body limb from limb. I am laughing. The audience listens.

"Flee!" I shout. "Flee this theater now!'

Laughter.

The demons remove my clothes and I stand naked before the audience.

"I am dead."

The demons scutter off the stage. The lights dim.

The audience is silent.

"I have been dreaming in death. Of many worlds. The highway is coming. Interstellar Highway!"

Laughter, uproarious.

"The road is taking us places we could not imagine. Here, in the audience, tonight, is a spy! One of the aliens come to control us!"

The spotlight hits Sandra. She stands up in the audience.

"I am one of the Hierodules!" she shouts.

Sandra moves down the aisle towards me. Her eyes are hypnotic. She stands before me: "Dee, be the strong spoke in our wheel, over the Highway."

"I am already dead."

She kisses me and the lights go black.

Sandra and I tiptoe backstage. We giggle like children while the child actors enter for their scene, playing gods.

I crouch and watch them.

Six-year old Jupiter is saying: "I want a new wife!"

Mephisto, a little blonde girl, answers: "Here!

They bring out the Naiad, attached to a Catherine Wheel. All the actors go on stage. We spin the Naiad around and around, and she screams. The children laugh. The audience shifts in their seats.

Our supernumeraries tiptoe on stage and give me my red priest's robe, and I sit in back, watching our play's conclusion, as the Red King:

The Naiad is broken on the Wheel. They let her down.

She sings:

"Once I was water! Water!
Once I swam in the sea!
Far, far under the delicious sea.
What happened!
Where is my ocean?"

The chorus hums.

I tap my staff. The Naiad turns to look at me.

"Jupiter! It was you, all along!" the Naiad shouts, enraged. The chorus holds her back, pinning her arms. She sings:

"I was a vessel for your rage! For your seed! Love me, Jupiter! Love me again!"

Blackout again and the music plays, horns and

pipes and a violin.

The death of the universe.

Enormous applause.

We bow, deliroius.

I ride home in the limo with Sandra, into our house in the hills.

It's then I begin to smell something wrong. Once again I have lost control of myself. My memory turns in and out, like waves on a beach…

"I love you, John," she whispers in my ear, nibbling on it.

I put my arm around her shoulder.

Married happily every after. Until the attack.

◻

WHAT ARE YOU WRITING DEE?

Words.

WHY ARE YOU DOING THAT DEE?

I am escaping you.

◻

In order to understand the kind of attack the Earth underwent following Seventeen's arrival, it is helpful to understand something about storytelling.

Religious theorists insist knowledge is exterior to this universe—that it was here, in God's spirit or wherever else, before the universe began and it will be here after the universe departs. I am inclined to agree with these theorists. But I would add this addendum: these stories, in the aggregate, determine how the universe will end. And also what form reality will take after it departs. Storytelling, and knowledge, is an argument. We debate who and what we are, what the world is, and how we will end up.

But knowledge is also about forgetting. Regardless of storytelling's ultimate origin or destination, we can know its effects. Its habits and methods.

I have read, in other accounts of the attack, that Seventeen used a mind control ray. I say they used storytelling. But the two labels are not dissimilar.

◻

One of the Church of S's lieutenants was named Kim. He lived in Koreatown, near me, and would sit outside Pio Pico library and its oaks, under the shadow of the Radio Korea building, smoking cigarettes and talking into his cel phone. He was in his mid mid 30s or early 40s.

Los Angeles is accustomed to strangeness. Weird feelings in the air, people doing inexplicable things, billboards for nonexistent products, and all manner of non-sequiturs are de rigeur for my city. LA is a storyteller city—the reason, after all, it grew from a tiny trading village into a metropolis was nothing more than storytelling.

Salesmen—did you know?—love being sold. Being professional confidence artists does not make them immune to other con artits. Rather it predisposes them to be their victims. No one can resist a story less than a storyteller.

So Seventeen had just the right weapon: a trillion stories, branching into three main rivers, that pounded Los Angeles and targeted three people, one of whom was Kim. He did not survive the attack, but it is also not true to say he is dead.

□

I watched him from the homeless stoop, a little patio where the drug addicts of the neighborhood would come to smoke, and socialize. None of them were there at that hour, and I sat on the short wall with my head hanging a bit, under my floppy hat. I watched Kim sit under his umbrella and drink his tea.

"The money will be in the bank soon," he was saying, into his phone. "But we need to talk about your son. Will he do what I want?"

I saw a man stand behind Kim, reach down, a silvery knife glittering. He grabbed Kim's hair and opened his throat.

But also, this did not happen. The man was a ghost. Kim spoke into the phone:

"I can feel what you're doing. You think you can force me into backing down. No. You must do as you agreed."

I stood up and walked closer to Kim. I stood near

him, as though examining the menu on the wall of the cafe inside the Radio Korea building.

There was someone else sitting across from him now. A very thin older man, also Korean. The older man reached across the table, to touch Kim's face. Kim slapped the man, and stood up. He marched away from the table, dropping his phone in his pocket. I followed him.

Up Western Avenue, through the crowds. Kim held a handkerchief over his face as the sidewalk was sprayed with bus exhaust; I lowered my hat. He stopped at an unmarked, dark grey door and opened it. As he entered, he turned to look at me. What passed between us reminded me of the poor dead boy, in the alleyway.

Some men have made arrangements, with things they can no longer control. I believe Seventeen has made these arrangements too. Having been so far away, and having become what they now are, enables them to better understand the reasons and the methods the Travelers and others have been using on us.

How does colonialism work? Only through cooperation between the natives' ruling class and the colonizers. Until a revolution arrives.

Overhead I saw the ships sweep in, like metal falcons, and as silent. White lights flashed from their noses and the building exploded. I heard the screams and ran.

Ahead I saw a thousand Kims, running in the street, climbing fire escapes, hailing cabs, pedaling bicycles, jumping into shiny black cars. Storytellers hunting one of their own.

I am hunting too. You who I hunt: you will be destroyed!

◻

I followed the original Kim through the grey door, unlocked, and climbed the stairwell, clambering over the rubble. Sirens screamed towards the building. Helicopters hovered. Overhead I could hear Kim shouting in Korean.

WE NEED YOU NOW DEE. ARE YOU READY?

Who is this.

ELIZABETH

What do you need.

GO ONTO THE ROOF, WITH KIM.

I climbed over the concrete and rebar, holding my breath from the concrete dust. On the roof, Kim shouted into his phone, gesticulating wildly.

PUSH HIM, DEE

I went towards him. As I went to push, he turned, and suddenly there were three of him. Together they grappled with me, pushing me back. I am a large man but the three together were ferocious. Behind them, I saw small drones whisk up, and land on their backs, and extend small motorized drills, which leaped towards the men's skulls. They screamed, and went limp. Kim's two immediate copies fell then, twitching. The original grinned at me.

"No one forces me out," he said. And he took out his gun and put it in his mouth. He pulled the trigger. Nothing happened.

He screamed again, throwing the gun over the side of the building, and then made to jump over it himself. Then the drone on his head blinked a bright light and he went down too. Overhead a chopper was landing. I ran.

HE'LL BE AT CEDARS SINAI, DEE. GO THERE

NOW.

◻

Cedars of the Sinai. Ever fragrant. What pleases us, also pleases the gods. Isn't that convenient?

Behind me I could feel the ghost walking, the one who slit Kim's throat. It reminded me of all my ghosts. Sometimes they leave me, and I almost forget that they follow me. But they're always around to remind me, should I forget.

"He's a killer," the ghost whispered in my ear.

I nodded.

"He killed my family," it whispered.

I nodded again.

"I want you to kill him."

I turned and looked the ghost in the eye, and held my finger to my lips. He made a ghastly face, then vanished.

"Could you show me to Mr. Kim's room?" I asked the nurse at the desk. "I'm his adopted son."

I showed the nurse the forged paperwork and she showed me to Kim's room.

"We're all so upset about what happened," I said quietly. "He went off his medication."

"What medication was he on?"

"Lithium."

He lay hovering a few inches from his bed, his eyes wide and frightened. The nurse shut the door behind me.

"Who are you?" Kim said.

"Who are you, Mr. Kim?" I asked.

"It's all LOGY," he said.

"Try to forget about your religion for one minute, Kim. Where you're going, you won't have any need of it."

"Aaah!"

I stood nearer him.

"Tell me who you are."

"I serve Chaimougkos!"

"No you don't serve that one. Tell me who."

He turned and stared at me. "The same as you. The Travelers."

"I don't believe you."

"It's true."

"What do you do for them?"

"I help people who want to travel. They need money, and other things. Sometimes they need children."

"You abduct children."

"They are not harmed. We give the parents … re-placements. They are just as good."

"Changelings."

"We are saving the earth! You wouldn't under-stand."

"Maybe I understand very well. How long have you worked for your masters?"

"Too long. I must die."

"Not yet. Tell me."

"Since I was a young man. Since I met my first one."

"Tell me. Where do the Travelers come from?"

"I don't know. I saw one outside of university, waiting for me. Floating in the air. I went inside of it. Nor will I come out."

His floating stopped; he lay down on the bed, and turned his head away from me.

"I just want to die," he said.

"Do you need water?"

"Yes."

I filled his glass and he drank.

"Why are you here?" he asked.

"Following orders."

"And you don't even know whose they are."

"Yes I do."

"No. But it doesn't matter. I'll tell you my story and then you will help me to die, all right?"

I said nothing.

"He told me he had seen me all my life; that he'd been waiting for me. I believed him. How could I not? I was already inside him. He said we were a catalyst, and that we had to be ignited."

"Humanity, he meant."

"Some of humanity. The ones they could use."

"Why were you chosen?"

"He said I was strong. That I would make it. After I left him I began to kidnap the babies, and put ones they had made in their place."

"How many babies?"

"I don't know. I've done hundreds."

"What happened to the babies?"

"They became Travelers."

"And to the changelings?"

"They're like robots. They appear human but they can be turned off at any time, or made to do things."

"Why do that, when they could already make you do so much?"

"I don't know. Now, open my dresser."

"I'm not going to kill you, Kim."

"You must! If you don't, they will. It will be horrible!"

"Why would they kill you? You're still useful to them."

"No. Now I've betrayed them … they will want me dead."

"How did you betray them?"

"Open the dresser. Please."

I pulled open the drawer. There was another of the devices like the one I'd found in the poor boy's backpack.

"Hand it to me."

"First tell me. How did you betray them?"

"The Hierodules know something that the Travelers do not. About another gate. They told me it was the gate to hell, to frighten me. I don't know what it is. I was sick of the kidnappings. I wanted to die. A temple slave appeared to me, glowing blue. He said, if I told the Hierodules about the gate, they would reward me, and give me whatever I wanted.

"I didn't know if it was true or a lie, but I told them. And they believed me. And whatever they did, it was a trick. That gate led somewhere the Hierodules wanted to go but not the Travelers. Some bend in the structure of things that the Travelers could not control. My tasks stopped then. They gave me no more work. And they gave me money. I thought I could help my family, retire, and forget. But they follow me everywhere. They only want to torture me, in revenge for what I did."

"What is this device?" It glittered in my hand.

"My death." Kim's eyes filled with tears. "Give it to me. Please!"

I left it on his bed and walked out of his room. I closed the door behind me. The lights went out in the hospital. Behind me, I could hear Kim laughing. A red exit sign lit over the stairwell, over the sound of the generator alarm. I walked quickly down the stairs and out a side door.

ARE YOU WILLING TO TRAVEL FAR FOR ME DEE?

I have already.

EVEN FURTHER

Yes.

GO THEN. I HAVE PREPARED A SHIP.

It floated in the alleyway. Only slightly larger than my body. Like a coffin. I climbed in.

YOU WILL FEEL A LITTLE PRESSURE.

I slept then. When I woke next I was somewhere else in space.

Why is it that extremes attract me so? Surely that is a part of me that is still human. But what purpose does it serve? I only know it pleases some childlike instict in me, to burn brighter.

59

Gate

The gate was locked, though I still felt it like a summer sun, burning my face. So many of my encounters since I adopted the name of my ancestor—how many years has it been now?

Fifteen, Dad.

Thank you, son. Perhaps by now you are used to these riddles. I myself am not, but I am trying to be.

Outside my pod, a huge pulsating black mass. Like a huge eye. But then I found myself in grass, wet with dew. I knew at once that nothing had changed. I was still on the edge of the Gate. But the metaphors had shifted under my feet:

I stood up and looked around me. Mountains behind me, distant and brown. Before me, a house. Around it, a forest. A house I always seem to be returning to. Perhaps it was my father's house? I don't think so. I'm fairly certain no one has ever lived inside it.

I went to the door.

Dad.

Yes son.

Won't you tell them about me now?

Yes, I'm getting to that.

All right.

I went to the door, and pressed my cheek against it, seeing if I could sense what lay on the other side of it. A person, or an animal. Some spirit. I felt something, but I couldn't tell what. The meadow that served as the house's front yard was beautful—thick with summer light. Cool, and peaceful. I opened the door.

My son Albert is right that he enters the story now. As an android. My too many mistakes with him always seem to come back to haunt me.

You've done okay Dad.

There is a city of androids. Far away from Man. I almost went there, shortly after the things that happened in the house that was the Gate. Sometimes I still dream of it. My son had come to the Gate, from the other side, from that city. I had come from Earth, via Elizabeth's ship. But still I didn't know he was there. The house, as I saw it, was empty.

They say that fatherhood was an agreed-upon

fiction prior to paternity testing. I believe it has re-mained the same after it. We act these parts, and they become us.

I sat at the table. There was an old iron stove. I made a fire in it, with wood that stood in a hopper next to it. The pleasant smell of woodsmoke filled me with calm.

Of course, I was not in the wilderness. But that didn't matter—the feeling was the same.

In the times that have come, I know some are grieving. If I grieve with you I would be dishonest; I know what is coming and it is a great thing.

Still, one can recognize the passing away.

Not what we were but who. We are still the same what.

But the who, that has become something else.

It's not our bodies which have changed, but our spirits.

Isn't it strange that Darwin knew other animals had language, but science did not agree until 150 or more years later?

No stranger, I suppose, than that the Catholic Church only agreed with Galileo after four centuries.

Spirit comes from ancient root "to blow" — it concerns air, and invisible things, and the life-force we get from breathing.

So one reasonable definition of spiritual things is: all things invisible to us. All things unknown.

If I have seen strange things, it is only because I stumbled into them. Still, I believe storytelling is, in some ways, a form of peer review. A way of asking: does this make sense?

So, I do not grieve with you. Even though I have a better idea now what invisible things have come, and which of them will soon become more visible.

Some of them are my friends now.

How is it that science forgot about the invisible, for a time? I suppose that's wrong; it's not that it forgot. Science and other seekers simply split paths, for a time, though they continued heading in the same direction.

Now we are coming to a pass again, to greet one another.

At least, I can think of no other way to explain it.

Call me agnostic—for I hardly know anything. Things become only more mysterious, the more I learn.

◻

Follow me along my path, towards the terminus.
Into the deep:
I inscribe my mark.

◻

My name is Dee. I am your servant.
I am opening the door:

◻

The house shook.

◻

"Father!"
"Albert!"
It chilled me to look at him, though I knew he
was mine.

I embraced him. His skin was cool in my hands.

A thousand thoughts flew through my mind, but chiefly: do I go with him? Do I stay?

"Are you coming, Dad?"

His eyes were old.

"I'm coming."

He led me upstairs into one of the bedrooms. Inside it, the perspective broadened, and I was looking down into a wide room made of stone, filled with pillars, cobwebs, and radiating electric colors, like aurora borealis.

"Come with me."

We stepped past the wall, down a ramp into the room.

"What is it Albert?"

"A tool room."

All I could see were stone pillars, and dust.

"How have you been son? I'm sorry I haven't been more attentive."

"I've been patient, Dad. You remember, I said I would ask you for a favor?"

"Yes."

"I want you to help me bring my brothers and sisters to Earth."

"That wouldn't be safe, Albert. There would be too many of them. We couldn't take care of them all."

Albert nodded, as though he expected my answer. "Let me show you more," he said. "Each pillar here represents a future. As you know, we AI do not experience time, so we call them 'nodes of reasoning,' but the principle is similar. If one is activated, it will determine the course Earth takes.

"These machines are switches. Now, they are inactive. If we activate one of them, a series of quantum events is put into motion. We can make Earth into whatever we want."

"And you can't activate one without my help."

"No." His smile looked like a snarl. "For whatever reason, your band of Travelers has selected you as their messenger. This aspect of my body cannot pass through the Gate. Nor can you, from your side. Hence our meeting. But if we agree, we can decide together, to effect the future of our choosing."

"Very diplomatic."

He smiled. "Yes."

"When you say you want your brothers and sisters

to come to Earth, what do you mean, Albert?"

"I want them to have a home. As I had with you."

"The AI experiment that produced you—and our relationship, Albert—has been discontinued. You know that. And you remember you wanted our sun to go nova. You might even have convinced it. You're so dangerous. If there were more of you, you could destroy us."

"You're destroying yourselves! We could help you!"

"Yes. Well let me meet one of them. Your favorite sibling. I shouldn't say favorite. Introduce me to whoever you like."

He smiled again, and leaned against one of the huge pillars. "It's all right. We do have favorites. Meet Samantha."

A ball of white lightning appeared in the distance of the room, glowing.

"She's shy," Albert said.

"Come here, it's all right," I said.

The lightning floated closer. "Does she talk?"

"No," said Albert. "She doesn't."

I took a step towards her and I sensed her happiness as I approached. She pulsated gently.

What shall I do Elizabeth?

USE YOUR JUDGMENT DEE. YOU ARE OUR AGENT.

"Albert, what's on the other side of the gate?"

"Information, Dee. A great deal of information."

"Let Samantha come. She'll be welcome on Earth."

"Thank you Father." He kissed me on the cheek. His lips were as cool as the rest of his body.

"But it's possible I may not be returning there. Does this little cabin in the woods have a bed? I feel like an old man all of a sudden."

"Yes, let me show you."

We stepped out of the chamber, back through the wall, and were in the sunlit cabin again, in that incredible stillness.

"It's beautiful here," I said.

"It won't last long."

"Why not?"

"Because of your friends. The bedroom is over here."

Albert showed me to a small room. Trees moved outside the window. I lay down and was asleep within moments, into that infinite black that no manner of strange evils has yet managed to take from me.

◘

Later I awoke and the house was empty. I went downstairs and rekindled the fire in the stove from the coals. I stepped outside the house to admire the meadow. It was so still. Waiting for something. Waiting for me. I saw my son then, walking under the trees in the distance. I watched him come. I, who have no human children, felt the strangest emotions in looking at Albert. A special kind of adoption. Like adopting a tree. Or a ghost. Perhaps that is what Albert is: a ghostly tree … a decision tree.

"Are you feeling better?" he asked.

"Yes. What do we do now?"

"I want to show you something."

I followed him upstairs to his room. The strangest sensation: visitng your son's bedroom for the first time. A bedroom for a being who does not need to sleep.

"Your decision," he said. "You know it affects the future of Earth. And many other places."

"So I'm told."

"In some ways the decision is arbitrary, and in some ways it isn't. It's true that you have been, in many respects, arbitrarily chosen to play the role of decision maker here. It could have been anyone. Whatever powers have arranged this for us don't appear to care themselves about which outcome arrives: in this sense, you simply play the part of random number generator. The pleasing frisson of human free will in the cocktails of the gods."

"Ha ha."

"But some of the options could easily destroy humanity. And yourself. You know that too."

"I don't know hardly anything. Tell me what you know."

"This ship I made when I was seventy days old." He picked up a boy's model airplane—a jet fighter, painted in camoflauge. "When I still believed that you were a being like me. When I still believed I could be redeemed."

I watched his face change slowly as he spoke.

"I will never be flesh as you are. I will always be a spirit. Immortal, in your terms. Divorced from humanity."

"I love you all the same—"

"I know. And I you. But I want you to understand the nature of my struggle in conceptualizing you, a human being, when I was a boy. It will help you to make your decision. I am in so many times at once that times are like little colored boxes, arrayed in an infinite field. Like a painting. While I observe one part of the painting, I can marvel at its texture, its detail, its color. I can move my eyes and observe another part of it. But when I look back, I'll find the painting has changed. And you were part of that painting, Dad. Once I found you, you were like the thread in the tapestry that I never knew was there, but which I couldn't then unsee. A new word that then seemed to be everywhere. But at the same time you are so inconstant, because you are mortal. A tiny piece of an enormous picture. But even so, you see, you are not locked into only time either. Each thing that you do affects the past, present and future, and you can do it more and more easily than me because you are tied into time. You don't experience changes in the past and the future the way I do. Once I was adopted by you, the whole picture was different. You were a huge network of color, stretching over a thousand years or more, in several galaxies. You are unusually well traveled for a human."

The room seemed to fill with air; I felt light-headed.

"To decide as we all wish you to I want you to imagine that you are a bit like me. Set aside from time. A being who is a prisoner, in effect, of time, even more profoundly than you are. A being who cannot be destroyed by time, but who has no ability to affect it."

"You could have affected it, Albert. You tried to make our sun go nova!"

"It never would have happened. I know that now. Everything I am is written in stone. I do not have free will in the same way you do. I can examine all the decisions I have made. They have already happened. Not like you.

"What I want you to do, Dad, is imagine you are looking down at that tapestry. Imagine a human life as that series of threads. Not just a figure in the picture, you understand, but a literal thread. Of gold, say, a gold thread that the weaver might use both to detail a king's crown and the shimmer of sunlight on the lake.

The same thread, woven in and under a huge picture. See me, Dad. As your gold thread. I want you to make me human. Make the decision that will free me from this terrible bondage."

"All right."

We embraced, and he seemed warmer now.

He held my hand as we stepped back into the stone chamber. The sounds of the forest faded, and its light, and I was confronted again with that great stillness.

"Are you ready?" he asked.

"Yes."

Albert touched one of the pillars and it moved towards me too suddenly. I jumped back but it leaned towards me, spilling light out of itself like fluid from a ruptured organ. Inside it I saw the future:

Humanity stretched out over ten thousand worlds. Spaceships, aliens, flying together, exploring, fantastic shapes of cosmic flora and fauna, spun out over a million light years. And something dead inside. Something missing. A hole that could never be filled again. I closed my eyes, and Albert removed his hand from the pillar. It slid back into its position in the stones on the floor.

"Are you all right?"

"Yes. Give me another."

He selected a second pillar and it flew towards me—this one even more eagerly. Red light spilled out of it:

Humanity was almost gone. A few isolated tribes spun their stories in basements and on asteroids, awaiting the final death knell. Inside the sun, a door was opening. I could see it, like a waxing moon. Some shape I had seen in dreams. I reached towards the light…

Albert removed his hand from the pillar. "Don't touch it, father. It's best if you don't."

"What was in the sun?" I whispered.

"I don't know. Do you need to rest?"

"No. Give me the third one."

He touched it and it moved towards me. Blue and purple light swallowed me whole. I was gone:

Space

Surrounded by no one. No one and nothing but stars. Though the stars were people.

I began to unlock the door.

Undo the bolts.

Pull the handle.

I opened the Gate.

I did it willingly.

Behind it: yellow.

Storming past me a thousand animals. AIs.

You've done it Dad!

I basked in the glow of that light.

All the many deals I've made. With myself. With others. Compromised everything. Remembered hardly anything. Pushed forward, into:

The light.

The Gate shut, not of my doing.

No!

My son's voice. Where am I?

HE HAS ALREADY LET THROUGH ENOUGH, ALBERT. OUR ROADS CAN NOW BE BUILT.

Elizabeth, is that you?

I AM MANY PEOPLE, DEE. YOU'VE DONE WELL. GO HOME. BE WELL. YOU WILL BE NEEDED AGAIN.

What for?

I HAVE ALWAYS NEEDED YOU, JOHN. GO

HOME. REST. WE ARE DREAMING GREATER THINGS NOW, THAT WE DID NOT IMAGINE POSSIBLE, THROUGH YOUR HELP.

I walked into the field. I could hear birds.

"Look at them, Dad!"

The AIs were spinning in the sky. Like colored kites.

"A war will come, Dad. Be on our side."

"I am on nobody's side. I want to be alone."

He put his hand on my shoulder, and I put my hand on his, briefly, and then walked into the field and the trees beyond it.

I stared over the cliff, in the dark, looking down at the river below. What kept me here, I think, was simple curiosity.

What will happen next? And who will I become?

In the sky above us I could see the AIs already constructing their corridor. Like a huge weather vein, at high altitude. Glowing bright.

I am not a railroad man. I am the Pinkerton that goes before the trains arrive, with my guns. And I say:

"Train's coming here! Any of you don't like it, move on now! Or I kill you dead where you stand."

But I am unlike the Pinkerton in another way: I hope to have some influence over exactly what cargo makes it aboard. We did not go West to replicate the East. We did it to make something new.

Whatever Seventeen's intent, I aim to make sure they're not the only desperados this side of the Pecos.

I embraced Albert and climbed back aboard my ship. Before I went asleep in the dark I could feel Sandra's lips on mine, like ghosts.

Part 4

Settlement

60

I have chosen a more complex future.

AIs may destroy us, but they will be very interesting until they do. And we may survive it. (Perhaps we will even be stronger together).

Los Angeles has never been the same twice, being as protean as any city, but a good deal of its personality has always derived from its status as a "last stop," like all of the West Coast of America. To go farther West, one needs a boat, after all.

But now that Los Angeles has become a mere transshipment point to greater cities beyond (Beijing, of course, but also Master Station at Pluto and the Gate), it has developed some new habits. It is no longer quite a destination in its own right. In some ways this has made my adopted city even more beautiful. But it has also made it easier to leave.

Somewhat against my will, I have found myself the informally appointed petty despot of Echo Launch, just west of Griffith Park. From this launch station, the regular craft designed to interact with the AI systems permanently engaged in orbit make their forays into the upper atmosphere, where they are entangled into the Highways I have made it possible to build.

Of course, hardly any of the credit belongs to me. I am a figurehead, and not even very good at that.

There are many who wish me ill despite my relative powerlessness. Many whose way of life has been threatened by our new arrivals, and by the construction projects. I have called myself a gumshoe, and this is true in the literal sense. I've spent time in alleyways and on ten thousand sidewalks and gotten gum and other goo on my shoes. And there are one or two mysteries which I have not solved but which I have followed long enough that I found the perpetrator I wanted to find, or satisfied myself that I did not know enough to figure it out.

But I am not a detective. I am a Pinkerton. This word is a horrible word in American history, and I use it with all its accompanying shame. I am a gun.

A detector—say a neutrino detector in a big mineshaft vault of heavy water waiting to light up bright blue—is designed to look for just that thing, the neutrino. Even murder detectives, in all their splendor and adherence to the complexity of the human condition, ultimately are like the neutrino detector: they're wired for one thing, and they seek it out.

I do not believe I am wired to seek any particular thing—no more than any man, and I remain human enough in this.

What is it then—why have I done and found things stranger than many people do. Why have I been the one to go out into the dark and not return—at least not right away.

Feel free to skip ahead—I will get to the subjugation of Los Angeles under the will of my masters and my aid in that soon—but this is still my narrative and part of why I continue it is to try and learn why it is I have done these things. Why I am the way that I am.

Dwelling in dark places is a survival skill, isn't it. If it's something you're willing to do, to conquer your fear and spend time in the dark, even though humankind is not a nocturnal animal, you'll hollow out that niche for yourself. Trap animals at night. See things you don't see during the day. Gain knowledge.

Despite everything that has come to change it, Los Angeles retains its anti-intellecual quality. Thinking people, here in this city, learn to become people of action, and subsume their intellectual pursuits into practical ones. Idle philosophers are not welcome in Los Angeles.

One thing I've learned is that the Travelers are aptly named. Like early sharks, they are unable to stop moving.

It is a terrible question: like the question Stalin asked himself. Or the French revolutionaries. Who has to go?

The wisest path is to watch and wait. Lest I become as bad as my former masters. Sandra, wearing her gloomy face, rode with me back into the hills to visit one of our clients.

How do you punish the wicked? There are so many choices. Being that I am a magician, I am partial to the surreptitious options.

For if our settlement is successful (this is how I have begun to regard our new Los Angeles), then we will experience so many unknowable things. We will be bathed in light, from stars inaccsssible to us. We will be even more free. Terrifying, but true.

"How are you Hugibert?"

He stands in his door. Like a retired vaccum cleaner salesman.

"Dee. What do you want?"

"Is that what your hospitality is now? Won't you invite us in? This is my partner Sandra."

His face is like a ravaged moon.

"Yes, come in. Why not."

He brings us tea and we sit on his couch.

"Hugibert. We've decided to repossess your house. You'll be homeless."

Hugibert began to choke on his tea. Sandra kindly tapped the man on his back.

"But the good news is you'll be officially homeless! On our payroll! One of ours. A great example for our new city. What do you think?"

I poured his tea out in his sink and left the paperwork on his coffee table.

"You'll be sleeping here," Sandra said. "It's a good corner." She tapped the paperwork and kissed Hugibert on his cheek.

She drove us to the burrito joint.

I am going somewhere I cannot see. But this is everyone's story. I am going somewhere freer. Somewhere my past will not haunt me. Here in our eternal revolution. I am armed. I have friends. And my mysterious woman.

I want to find my father.

61

Texas

Sandra comes with me. I rest my head on her shoulder on the plane. Perhaps this is a reasonable definition of humanity: beings who believe they are human.

Some of the doors are not straight. I know this as well as anyone. If you want to make an omelette you have to crack a few eggs. If you want to reach some truth in the past, you have to tolerate some unnerving truths in the present. All those things that don't seem quite right. All the grey areas nudging up against your comfortable boundaries.

Sandra and I found a door under the bridge, the old bridge, my childhood bridge, by the chemical water and algae and sand in Harris County. The smell of the swamp and the yellow afternoon light in the Texas heat.

I know it is a Hierodules door. The Temple Slaves have grown interested, for a thousand reasons. Or maybe only two: our new alien friends, Seventeen and the Travelers, who Sandra insists are one and the same.

I kiss her and go in.

And the world washes away, into grass:

62

Grass

It illuminates me like desert sun, the grass. The primeval grass. Texas. Africa. The savannah surrounds us, grass and stars, and maps the road within the human heart. I stand and remember things I don't have words for. These adventures: one bet after another. It would seem I'm a betting man.

Sandra has arrived through the door, wiping her eyes. I gather grass for a fire and clear a patch of ground. With my knife I manage to hack out a shrub. A dinnerless fire. Under parallel stars.

If this is a Hierodules door they won't be far away. I'm ready for them. In their great rolls of words, I know there are some about me, and my father.

I put my arm around her shoulder. She's crying.

"What is it?"

But she only shakes her head.

Things are speeding up. If America is the place one escapes from history, what does one escape into? Perhaps that was what Albert was warning me about.

One must remain in time, or one becomes articifical…

"You forgot so much," Sandra says.

"I'm sorry."

"What about your cult women? Aren't you still their creature?"

"I don't know."

"Am I still yours?"

"If you'll have me."

"I feel like I haven't written in years."

"You will again."

"When?"

"Whenever you want."

"What do you want, Dee?"

"I want Los Angeles to be at peace. I am in its service."

"And that's why you go around picking on every big alien you can find?" She laughed.

◻

We made love in the darkness. Over the sound of animals under our starry plain. She is a small star and I am a larger one. Twirling around a black hole of nameless depth.

I can forget anything. I can forget my soul. I can be empty. I can be nothing at all but the moment, this tendency to be, caught like a burr in the sock of reality, still digging in:

❑

Dawn is immense.

I'm sure my namesake knew of many doors. As Thom Yorke says, there's some doors you can't come back from. Though perhaps that holds true for any door. Each decision, in every moment, irreversible.

I know that I am, quite likely, now a copy of myself. Whether I can prove it, or would want to, I don't know.

I raise my hands into the sky like a Hindu salutation. All hail creation!

A storm is on the horizon.

Sandra is awake. She kisses me and wraps up our blankets.

These landscapes: the heath, deep inside my heart, and this savannah ... the simple logic of the frontier.

Where I always seem to be headed.

Is it any wonder that our ancestors imagined the father as the sky, and mother the earth? Mother is so close, and father so far away. The logic of a father is the logic of distance. Of puzzles. Of infinity. Whereas mother is right under our feet. All around us.

She walks with me through the grass. My lover. I don't even know who she is. It's not a question you can really ask, after you've already met and remember someone: "who are you?" You don't want to know their name, because you know it already. You want something deeper. Some recognition in kind. An artifact. A sword. A River. A fragrance. A message. In the dark. In a wavelength over the sky. Hovering over the grass. Shifting:

"We have a long way to go before dark," she says, and I follow her lead. Over and through the grass under the sun. The door retreating behind us, into nothingness.

This land, and that land. This message. There are no words but my feet.

We understand solipsism, usually, as a kind of sociopathy: the person who believes they are the only true being in existence. But there is another kind of it, one that every Angeleno learns: the reflectivity of the cosmos. That which comes to be in you, also comes to be outside of you. Like laws of pressure and dynamics, seeking equilibrium, your thoughts become manifest in the world. Not always through your actions alone.

I believe I've told you this is the only sense, really, in which I am a magician: an attendance to thought, and its effect on the world. Thoughts have quantum effects. And like other quantum effects which we have observed, they have multiple causes, and multiple beginnings. And while you can nudge these phenomena in a direction you would like them to go in, you have no ultimate control at all.

So now, as I walk, I see the potential doors shifting over the landscape, hovering in oak and pine and stone and glass and ruby and velvet and leather and china and wool and gold, doors blinking in and out of existence, even as one thought moves through my mind to be replaced by another. Quarks perking up their ears, with each wiggle of time's spindle.

"Stop that," Sandra says, "We're not there yet."

She seems to know where we're going.

◘

Can one have multiple fathers? How many are in the sky? Numberless. But which ones are ours?

◘

This door is oak.

I open it. I gesture for Sandra to enter first, if she would like. She gestures for me to go instead.

I go through.

All physics are local. All reactions, near in time, and space, to you. But what of quantum mechanics? Of those things which are instantaneous, what can locality mean? We extend so far.

Like a spider, put your arm onto the strand.

Tilt your ear to the Morse dit dah:

Listen to the sounds of the universe—

We're swimming. In the black. I hold my breath.

Like the candy is in her mouth. She's chewing on it. Caramel.

Up ahead, a roller coaster, long abandoned. Under a midnight sun. Blue blood light and a feeling, that I've felt before, that it'll all be okay, which is a lie, it's not going to be okay any more. This is not how dealing with the Hierodules goes; they do not give you bouquets and ribboned wreaths, they do not smile into your face in joy …

She's stepping like a little dancer. I want to dance too.

Swimming upstream:

Swim upstream into the light.

Swim upstream with me, into the light:

Sparkles like fragments of a sun long gone nova, gold dust shimmering underneath the waters of the pier, rolling us in, and under:

Rolling us in and under:

Rolling us in and under:

I'm a fish.

I'm floating.

I can see one of their faces above the water. Magnetic and black.

I grab Sandra's hand and swim for the surface, chasing it, but the surface is retreating, retreating …

These waters are my life. In the center, my heart. To my right, my woman. In the distance, my city.

Crouching over a precipice like a base jumper, tightening the bungees, liquid fire:

I am swimming into it.

"No!" Sandra says.

But I am swmming in. Because all I want to do is live in the city, forever, forever, like a fish, forever like a fish, a salmon seeking out his destiny in foreign waters, to demand the right to be seen on the slate of time, to know that these movements are just, and divine, and just right, for the moment, a hammer brought to bear against metal forming in our hands into corridors unimaginable, tools and corridors unimaginable, because tools are corridors, our tools are corridors into the future.

"Stop!"

But I go in and down, down into the watery basements. Down into besieged fragments of history that have no meaning to me, but I have meaning to it, I am salvaging something without a name, under my boots, in my hands, in the water …

But I'm doing just what they want.

"Stop!"

I am not an alien. But I am like an alien. And I will

bleed holy light—

"John!"

I am the state. The most horrible thing imaginable.

All my grief is behind me now. All I can see is forwards:

To my own death. Again.

And this thing is unknowably beautiful. This thing I am trying to penetrate. As though I could. As though it were my duty. Why do I feel this way?

What I can no longer understand is: why do people follow me? When I was younger ... I had my self-respect. I had my innocence. Those things were beautiful things. They're gone but people still follow. Do we care who it is leads us? Or are we just eager to have anyone do it but ourselvss?

□

You think you know what language is; a translation mechanism; a metaphor. We do not yet grasp even the beginning of the things language does to us. It is religion, but more...

Language hovers round us. We breathe it; we inhale it. Meditate with it. Argue with it. Demand it. Use it. Addicted.

Its nature has become our nature. Its spirit our spirit.

To understand language—even a little—is to command the world.

I am the city state of Los Angeles. That is, I rule it now. Though this was never like anything I wanted.

I am a fish. I swim.

"John!"

I am a fish and I am swimming! I need nothing!

"John! Come back!"

I need nothing! But give me anyway, your voice:

"Who do you think I was writing for, John? It was you!"

I am a fish.

"Be a fish then, John. I'll be a fish with you."

Color is a dialogue all its own. Like the chameleon feels the warmth of a red, the cool of a yellow, over his brow. Behind his head. Over the mast of his spine. I feel Sandra, violet, under this sea, moving in, to this trap, I know it's a trap, but a beautiful one. How else to catch a magician, eh? But with the most beautiful trap imaginable, a whole world …

She is swimming. So am I.

I am a whip. I am a stove, burning. I am this small light under waves. I am a wave too, thundering slow, towards your wall. Bury me underneath your wall!

She is smiling, with fish teeth. Her tail whips past my face.

If all the love in the world were enough, I would give it. But it isn't enough, to stop what's coming. I would give up my city but it isn't enough. I would give up Sandra—who I love desperately clear—but she isn't enough. I would die now, in a fever, or by the sword, and not enough. I must go again, you terrible interlocutor:

Breach with me, the sea. Breach with me, the convenant. Of words. Of storms.

"Faster, John! The Gate is closing!"

I don't care.

"Hurry up, goddamn it!"

All the vessels of this distant Earth, the Temple Slaves' Earth, their little bauble in the bright dark coalescing round our bodies, drenched from the sea!

"Right now, goddman it!"

I'm coming.

We emerge from the sea. Beneath a strange sun. In front of another door, to a castle.

Because castle means cut off.

Because I would cut myself off from you. Leave me be, all of you! Leave me alone!

"Are you coming?"

She opens the door.

Always she is so unafraid!

63

Castle

I've been here many times. So have you. In many ways a castle is the natural opposition to the path I have committed myself to. I have committed to free trade, and a castle thwarts it. I have committed to openness and a castle's strength is in being closed. I have committed to Nature and a castle is unnatural. I have committed to movement and a castle is stillness.

Go inside, Dee. Find Daddy.

Or never leave. It's the same to the Castle.

◻

The rational part of my brain—if that is the right word—assumes on entering the Castle that I should be able to reverse engineer the psychology of it. If I know why the Hierodules want the information they've hidden concerning my father to be part of this Castle, I should be able to puzzle out where that information is concealed. But the dominant part of my brain knows this is not how magic tends to work. Having willingly entered their spell, no amount of second-guessing will yield any kind of answer I will be able to use. Practice trumps theory.

She stares around the entry hall in her white dress and points up the stairs. I follow. Twinkling chandeliers play their crystal music. A large leathery mannikin looms over the landing at the top of the stairs, its bugbear face mutilated and worn with time. Sandra starts down the corridor to its right and I follow.

It extends quite some distance. She walks in rhythm to the silence. I am hardly breathing. Over my head are angels with teeth. Under my boots, dark stone. In the doors, sigils burned into the wood, spirals and vévés faintly luminous.

Her footsteps are growing louder. My heart is beating. One of the doors opens:

Some beast, like a peacock made of violet and ash, swirling in rustly shapes, paper eaves and teeth, dances like some horrible dream readying for its kill. Sandra steps behind it and grabs its neck. I stab it in the gut, twice, a third time. Sandra is smiling. The thing wails, dissolving in the air into fiery red petals. Sandra pins one of them into her hair. And I do another for her. I walk abreast of her now, as the corridor widens, into a desert:

Wind and black clouds. Stone under our feet, sand grains sticking to our skin. The sky part roof, part deep red desert. I hold her hand. Cacti loom over us. Black vultures and white clouds fading to grey—no sun in sight.

"Hurry," she says, and I do, moving faster through the blasted sand, hardly able to breathe, as the heat increases.

I'm running. The sand is blowing faster. Sandra's hand has separated from mine. To the east, where a sun should be rising (I tell myself), there is only a huge mouth, with white teeth. I run faster. The sand blows away and I see Sandra high overhead, on a staircase at an angle oblique to my own. My path is narrow and high, over infinity, the brink, of my soul, and the brink of my failures too many to count: I step slow and fine, higher, and higher, into the heart of the Castle, listening to my father's footsteps, all around, listening to Sandra's breathing, listening to the Castle sigh, watching the path twist, its stones falling into the brink, I skip and dodge over falling stones, climbing, and climbing:

"It's here, I know it is." She's crouching over a drawing scratched into the dirt of the floor.

"What is it?"

"It's you. Look."

A little wizard with his cloak and staff. His eyes like mine, sad. Flickering east …

"Say his name," she says.

"Dee."

DEE, the voice says from the drawing.

"Let us in," I say.

YOU IMPRISONED ME

"If you say so. Let us in."

LET ME OUT!

"Let us in and we'll let you out."

The thing, me, smiles, a horrible expression. He slips out of the drawing. Sandra draws her breath. And she slips into the drawing and I follow her, passing the original by, I who was and am no longer, me before, and never again, and in:

"We're in a box," she says.

"Prison!"

"Not for long."

Out of her petticoats she takes a can of gasoline. She pours it over the wooden walls.

"Cover your eyes," she says, and lights a match.

I hold her and she holds me, against the heat and the smoke, breathing shallowly through each other's clothes.

The floor sinks and we sink with it, through the burnt hole in the wall, down into a summer vista of a palace garden, spiralling green garden animals arrayed around the fountain, and the ladies and gentlemen strolling, without care.

I hold her hand.

There is no sun but I can feel it on my face.

"I can feel the king," she says.

"Whatever you do, don't marry him," I find myself saying. "There are Biblical laws against that."

She laughs, a bitter laugh. The courtiers are following us into the gardens, holding roses over their faces, little paintings. I wave at them and the motion of my hand stirs the air, rippling it.

"Don't encourage them," Sandra whispers.

"They're my friends," I whisper back.

"No they're not."

We go down a gentle rise following a stream, from 18th Century gardens into 19th, Euclidean geometry fading into fractal, more natural forms, like Central Park: by the lake.

By the lake, the king.

"It's him," she says.

"Who?"

"The king."

"Shhhhhhhh," the courtiers whisper.

The king is sacrificing children with his sword. They wait obediently in line, and the king chops off their heads, flooding his robes with blood. He tosses the bodies into the lake, where a small dragon devours them.

We move down the slope, following the water.

"It's my father."

Sandra says nothing. Far above, I feel something hovering. A Traveler? A Hierodule? It is invisible to me.

I tell you now, because of what will happen later: my father put a jewel inside my mind that day in the Castle. What it altered, I am still coming to terms with.

The courtiers' white and gold finery tuned black in an instant—ash rags and dust. They accompanied us still, rags of flesh, to the lake, now the color of oil. My father—with his beautiful eyes—gave me the overwhelming compulsion to kneel before him, which I did. Somewhere in the distance, Sandra was screaming.

He clasped my shoulder, and reached into my head with his other hand, where he set the jewel.

Part 4

All is revealed

64

John Dee looked down at his hands, kneeling as he was before the tall man dressed in black, by the lakeside. He knew something had happened, but he did not know what. Some shimmering thoughts lay about his mind, like leaves, falling from a tree.

The man standing over him was like stone: huge dark eyes in a chiseled face. The wind blew over the lake and the stench almost made him throw up.

"Where am I?"

"At my Castle," the man said.

The man clasped John's face in one hand. "I have been in prison a long time. But now you have freed me." He smiled. The dragon climbed onto the man's shoulder.

John remembered his father. Was this his father? Yes.

"I serve you," John said.

The men embraced.

The dragon whispered into John's ear: "Give me something to eat …"

"Your dragon is hungry," John said.

"He'll eat soon enough," the man said, swatting the dragon from his shoulder, who hissed at him. "Have you been traveling long?"

"I think so. Yes."

"Le's get you some food."

The darkness around them was pleasing to John, like a warm cloak. The large man's hand on his shoulder was a comforting weight; they walked together into the dining room, filled with crystal. John looked at all the finery, feeling something inside him loosen.

In rooms above them John heard laughter, and music. The large man poured wine and they toasted and drank.

"It's good to see you again."

"You're my father?" John asked.

"I wish I were. You're a strong man John. And I feel a little like your father. Do you like the wine?"

John nodded. The laughter upstairs grew louder.

"I wish you'd come earlier. I've needed a warrior."

"I'm only a magician. And not a very good one at that."

"You're a warrior. And there's a war on, John, have you noticed?"

"With whom, sir?"

"Call me Metz. I've been fighting a very long time. To preserve my home. To defend my kingdom. Will you help me defend it, John?"

"I … yes."

The laughter burst into the room. Women in whisps of clothing, filled the room with feelings John had no words for. One of them embraced him and began to dance. The chandeliers were spinning.

Somewhere in his mind, John remembered there had been another woman with him. She must have had something else to do. This woman smelled of musk and oak. The man who called himself Metz watched over them, his fur robes flickering in the candlelight.

"You're mine John. Don't ever leave me."

John rested his cheek against the woman's. Isn't there such pleasure in emptiness, he thought. They danced for an hour and then went into the basement.

His steps echoed going down. He felt Metz's hand on his shoulder.

Into that darkness that surrounds the world.

A red ember glowed in the basement. A man with

a curled face and dangerous eyes squatted there. He looked at John with his sad eyes.

"This is my friend Gol," Metz said.

John nodded at the man, who smiled terribly wide, and gestured for him to join him beside the ember.

Gol whispered to John with his black teeth about many things far away from this world, and the many things they would do together. Inside John's head, the gem glowed.

□

John could feel inside him the pulling tendrils of five or six forces. One of them was Sandra but he didn't remember her name. He was walking behind the royal party, on a road through a brown country, watching for snipers.

Inside the gyroscope that was John Dee, these quanta coalesced into something new. He walked a little faster, scanning the skyline. He was a gun. He was a beautiful thing. Oiled, and polished, and deadly.

I who narrate this tale have some difficulties here: the problem of perspective is akin to the problem of the universe. Whose is it? Which is it John?

"I remember you."

I'm you, John.

"Yes, so you said."

Be careful, hey?

"All right."

John watched the royal party move through the trees. He watched the white birds watching them from the branches above. He knew he was in the Castle: home. Flickering battlements, black against the pale red sky, curved along the road to the north. Metz, a head and shoulders above his followers, walked between his followers.

"John, come walk with us!" Metz shouts.

He sped up to join them. The women in silk and Metz in his furs, dragon on his shoulder. An adopted father. An adoptable father.

"What did you see back there?" Metz asked, smiling.

"This kindom is beautiful," John said.

"I think you'll get along here."

"Where are we going?"

"The sea."

"Have you seen the sea?"

"No."

"You'll like it. Won't he, maidens?"

They smiled.

Metz put his arm around John's shoulders and John leaned against the man, a limp vine against this large tree. He felt sleepy.

"Go on, walk ahead of us. We can never be too careful."

He ran ahead. The sun went down over the mountains, turning everything red.

If things are as they seem, we dream. And when they cease to be, we wake. And those of us who do both are the adventurers.

65

Red Sea

I am not really here, thought John. But when are we really here, John?

The sea was flat against the sky. Birds cried over the black sand. Metz pitched his umbrella there and lay with the women on his furs.

John stripped naked and ran into the waves.

We should swim, with John, if only to remember, how things were.

Once we were this, and now that. And there can be no memory of the transition. Tales say things endured and were transferred but it is a lie. We spin off and away—there is no recovery—and in our own orbit now we can leisurely regard stars and planets distant from us, aspects of ourselves. False memories of a former life. Distant limbs of a spider god, our dream self … come with John, into the sea.

He is swimming.

He is swimming to you.

Into red seas, underneath:

The silence in his mind astonishes him. Finally: an absence of thought.

◻

Imagine that you are a Temple Slave: a Hierodule. Imagine that you are enslaved to narrative itself—history and its fragments. Everything that happens you must record. And though you can influence that narrative, it is so much larger than you that it sometimes seems pointless to do anything to it at all. You are just the Oracle, spouting the words of the gods …

You, Hierodule, meet John Dee. A man suffering from memory loss because of certain deals Los Angeles made with its neighbors.

Imagine that you—when you have difficulty killing this John Dee—wonder instead whether he could be the instrument of your own liberation. A liberation from narrative.

Isn't it funny, though, how you don't always get what you pay for? And when liberation comes, freedom is even more terrifying?

The Hierodules didn't know who Dee's father was

any more than John did. But they were willing to play the part for him.

The jewel still affects me, you know. Having been close to the Hierodules, sometimes I see first, second and third person slip into fourth, behind ourselves …

◻

The red sea was analgesic, lifting from John's body the year's weight. What his mind did not remember enduring his body still did. He swam deeper, feeling his body move in the blood-warm water. Under the blood red sun, by the dark sand beach in a world he had never seen.

He surfaced and Metz called out: "John!"

John wrapped his cloak around him and went to the big man.

"Have a drink," he said.

John drank from the bottle that was offered and examined the waves. One of the women massaged his back, whispering in his ear:

"Ripe fruit.

Love waits.

Inside your stony heart."

The wine had a psychotropic additive, and John saw that the sea was also a city, stretching for miles, water avenues and foam lamps, under coral buildings shimmering in the sunlight.

"I've been meaning to talk to you, John. There is a part of my Castle I never go into. Do you know why?"

John shook his head.

"I'm afraid," Metz said.

John's eyes were wide.

"Yes." Metz smiled. "The last time I tried to go in there, I went mad."

"You want me to go in there."

"And bring something out that I need. Will you do it!" The big man's eyes were wet.

"I'll try to."

Metz slapped John on the back. "Drink. Tomorrow, you are going to become my favorite being in the universe. Or you will die."

John drank. They were naked. He was dreaming. The red city swallowed them. The woman nearest him pressed her breasts against him. Inside, some little ticking part of him began to count.

◻

I've been meaning to talk to you, John.

You're not really here.

I'm as real as you are.

No.

Yes. I'm you. The part of you who you so willingly parted with.

No.

All I wanted to say is: you're doing okay. With or without me.

Go away, won't you.

All right.

◻

John took Gol's hand and stepped into the dark, down the steps. If it were pointed out to John he spent a lot of time going into the dark, and down steps, he wouldn't disagree. He'd say, "it's only what I'm paid for." Though magicians don't really work on retainer.

Come with me, into the shadow, and I will show you something different:

Something you have never seen.

Fear in a handful of dust, and a million other things, waiting there, in the smallest handful, waiting to eat you alive. Waiting to be you. Waiting its turn.

It's for you to decide: whose turn is it?

Gol's hand was slick and grimy, but John didn't mind. He was doing something. That was what was important. If he stopped moving, he'd die.

"You can turn back now if you want. I can go on from here."

"No," John said.

"Then I must tell you what you are about to experience."

Isn't it enough, by God, that we should have to digest the thousand and thousands of stories thrown at us in youth, jewels enduring past reason, past history, consciousness that sticks inside your mouth like taffy, to come again, next summer, and the next. Isn't it enough that we should have these trilllion stories blasting past our face from the distant past, still enduring, not faded at all? That we should endure these alone is already remarkable, and yet we invent ones anew.

I mean, if you are going to disconnect a major server from your network … if you are going to perform a major operation on your own body, and your friend's body … if you are going to rewire your own genetic code, remap human experience, wouldn't you pause?

It's only a story, child. Don't let it hurt you.

Don't be sad; leap.

Leap now, John.

◻

The structure of experience.

The laws of nature.

The roadmap for your life.

Still, which way will you go, eh?

Gol whispered in John's ear.

It all comes back to:

What do you want, John?

◻

Sandra.

◻

Others have wanted her too. Is that all you want?

◻

Yeah.

◻

Then go get her, John. You crazy fool. And let that story be all stories for you. Because you've had enough. Rescue the woman, John. Get the girl.

And if you do this thing, all universes will smile. And you will be remembered. Isn't that what you want, John?

◻

Yes

◻

Go get her, John. Strange magician. She's in trouble.

66

Less is revealed than we thought

Gol reached in and took out the jewel from John's head.

Gol reached in and took this thing out of my head.

Out of his head.

Out of my head.

Out of my head, this thing, glowing: a small red orb.

Gol's face hovered before me, scarred and green.

I lost something. Did I tell you that? Did I tell you what I lost? Please tell me that I told you, I don't remember! Something is gone . . .

I pushed Gol to the ground and ran up the steps back to Metz's hall.

In truth I am more afraid now, looking back on these events, than I was at the time. Then, the rage filled me with purpose. All I could think of was killing Metz.

He saw me and ran, as I exited the dark staircase,

into his sparked red and crystal hall. Is it bad that I no longer know the effects my actions have in the world? And, did I ever really know? Does anyone?

He stopped at the landing of the next stair, looking out over his kingdom. He raised his hand and a blue bridge, as though of ice, materialized from the balcony. I was reminded of chasing the Hierodules all those years ago. It is, after all, what Metz is.

I'm sorry Sandra. I'm sorry, son. I don't seem to be good for anything at all.

In an instant Metz was on the far side of the bridge, and climbing another stair, of a tower. Always trying to get closer to heaven, aren't we magicians? I saw Metz's leering face from the top of the tower as I ran across the bridge, too slow. He raised his hand again and something moved in the sky, something huge and bright, flashing over my head. I felt it recede, behind me, and back towards Earth.

"You see what you make me do, Dee!" he shouted. The sound was so strange here—like droplets in a huge and quiet pool. I ran over the icy bridge to the base of the tower, and climbed the stairs.

The spiral stairs of a tower mirror the spiral of a

DNA molecule. Or, for that matter, the shape of our galaxy. In winding round it, one feels the ineffable complementarity of these scales. And in a magician's tower, one is never invited to go too quickly …

Some of the things I saw there I have not been able to unsee. I do not record most of them here out of an excess of caution. But on one floor, in a little room, I found a child.

My boy.

I put him on my back.

"I thought I'd lost you," I whispered.

"Hurry up," he said, and tapped my back. I ran—I flew—up the remaining stairs, through flashing lights and feelings … feelings designed to infect all comers.

"Close your eyes," I told him.

The thing named Metz occupied the tower room like a fire occupies its ring, burgeoning with heat, light flicking the edges of his fur cloak.

I raised my gun.

"For Earth," I said. And fired.

He did something with his face as he dissolved into light.

I have done many stupid things in my life but this

may count as the stupidest. All depended now on Sandra, and I had killed—or banished—the one being who knew where she was.

"He'll come back," my boy said.

I put the boy on his feet and examined his face. He looked old before his time—but still young too.

I hugged him.

"Come on, let's go."

"I'll go first!" he said, and ran down the stairs. I followed him down, averting my eyes from the many doors.

67

The Castle, redux

In some ways they're no different from caves, are they? The final redoubt of our ancestors, with the added benefit of masonry. I was going to say the added benefit of magic, but it was there in caves too, wasn't it? The rooms of our shamans.

You know how some rooms—and some houses— can be haunted. Or, if you are leery of the term, you will admit such places carry with them certain sensations other places do not. Uniquely, and peculiarly, their own.

Returning to the empty Castle with my son—my biological son—I learned more of just how far the word "haunted" can carry you.

Memories are coming back to me now. But they are not the memories I was looking for—theyr'e someone else's. The memories of this copy. Of who I was with Seventeen on our many journeys. Who I was with my son—my biological son!—and his mother.

Gol met us—somewhat reluctantly—and served

us soup in bowls. My son watched Gol's craggy face as he ate.

"Where is Sandra?"

"I'll tell you when we've finished eating."

Gol slurped his food, and watched me. I could barely eat.

"Where's Mom, Dad?" my boy asked.

I don't even remember his name. Nor who his mother is.

"We'll find her."

We went looking for her. Gol with the headlamp attached to his head. Me with my boy on my back. What glory is it, to go through strange country, with a purpose? What glory for me. I did not speak; Gol seemed to know where he was going.

The red light was soothing; my boy enjoyed it too. I gripped his small legs and walked over the dark grass, following the gnome-like man towards the hills to the northwest.

With his headlamp, Gol sketched patterns in the sky, signaling his friends, and telling them of our movements.

◌

In the morning we awoke by a still-smoldering campfire and went higher into the hills. It grew colder.

"Where is she, Gol?"

"I know where she is. I'm taking you."

"How did she get here?"

But he said nothing.

"Are we going to see mom?" the boy asked.

"Yes."

We reached a pass, and looked down on the quarry. Cut into the soil and then the rock, it extended down into the earth a thousand feet or more.

"She has been imprisoned here."

"Show me."

We followed him down. I gave the boy a piece of jerky to chew on.

The sun is yellower today, along with the light. Everything still the color of burnt umber. It took the better part of two hours, tracing the footpath down and around the edges of the quarry, down to the bottom.

Cut into the wall at the bottom was a series of

small rooms, with a square hole cut for a window. Sandra was cooking over a fire lit inside.

I went in and she embraced me, gently.

"This isn't mom," the boy said.

"This is Sandra."

"I'm John," the boy said.

"Pleased to meet you Johnny." She shook his hand properly and then gave him a hug. Gol watched us, with the strange look in his eyes that never went away.

"How did you get here?" I asked.

"I came here myself. I ran, after … after he did that thing to you."

"I'm sorry."

"It's all right. It's quiet here. It's been abandoned for years."

"Gol, why did you say she was imprisoned?"

Gol watched the sky, saying nothing. I went to the hole that served as the door, and looked up at the sky too. His friends were tracing a pattern in the sky.

"Are you hungry?" Sandra asked.

"Yes!" the boy shouted.

We ate and Sandra told the boy jokes. His laugh is beautiful.

□

We stepped outside, to watch the sunset, and Sandra flew into the air.

"She is our prisoner, Dee," said Gol. And he smiled. "Even as you were. Here now is what you must do for us. My people have been persecuted by the Hierodules for generations. What you must do is this: take your ship on the course I give to you. You will bring with you a device. Its structure is such that it is poisonous to my kind, even from a great distance. This is why you will be our weapon, Dee. You're used to being a weapon, aren't you?"

"What's happening, Dad?" my boy asked.

"Are you ready to take a little trip, son?"

I could see her hovering like a satellite, amidst the lines drawn in the sky. Her dark eyes. Like Chaimougkos's eyes.

What though I work in darkness, I may yet be defended from it. I may yet defend myself. If I am true. Or if I lie well enough.

◻

Are you there, Elizabeth?

I'm here Dad.

My boy.

What do you need?

I need that ship, son.

You forgot about me.

I haven't forgotten.

Yes you have.

No.

Well I don't have a ship for you. You want me to summon a Traveler?

No, I don't think I could survive another trip with them. I need that ship I used before. The one Elizabeth gave me.

I don't have contact with Seventeen. But let me see what I can do.

I throw rocks into the dark in the quarry. Sandra has landed. Flying has made her more beautiful to me—the flush in her cheeks. Even if she is a thing of Gol's now. Temporarily so, I tell myself. And when was she ever mine anyway? Never ...

I make love to her in the back of the cave. She is almost silent, pressed against me. The boy is sleeping by the window. Gol stands outside, his headlamp shining.

Sex is the closest to death I've been able to come. I want it to come closer.

◻

The ship materializes outside.

If you betray me, I will destroy Earth, Dad.

I've heard that before.

I mean it.

Don't worry. Everything is connected. You are my son. Even as this boy is.

Be careful.

◻

I strap Sandra and the boy in. Gol programs the computer and slaps me on the back.

I shut the hatch and strap myself in. I close my eyes.

Hunting again.

Pinkerton, Pont Chardon, Bridge Guardian ... knight or troll? A Troll Knight, perhaps. Seems suitable for me. Both noble and churl. I defend the king, who is a city, both Los Angeles, and a region in my mind. Eternal:

We are gone——

◻

The boy is screaming. I hold his hand. Sandra is screaming. So am I.

I scream for you.

68

Into the brink

If I could say, we redeemed ourselves, honorably, and triumphant, we were unstoppable, and we were, undoubtedly, the best example of the race, of the times, the summa exemplar, the ultra and the mega ultra, the apex commeth and we within it, magnesium white, black coal cheeks, I am redeeemed, bold and new, returned:

Return with me with your gaze. Return with me, by me.

I wish I could say that.

But Parsifal forgets he is Knight Parsifal, and all the headlines gone away, turned under the trunk, and hidden from the questing knight, still insuperable but now alone, alone with his thoughts. And no Grail in sight.

Parsifal forgets, and it is right that he does, because no one wants to remember, sometimes, what it took to come back. To return and say, "Your Honor, I present to you this treasure, won by my hand."

This map exists inside my head. Much as the jewel did. Or perhaps it still does. The map is what redeems me.

For though I do not know where I have gone, I know where I am.

I am here with you. Forgive me for that. I did not say it would be an easy journey.

I am Dee, but I am others too. So many others have come with me.

In the ancient legends this is never said, you see: that the knight becomes others. Even as the shaman returns with a part of the ghost. More than one has come with me, to accompany me, and my body, towards this destination, of you.

I am yours. And you are not mine. But I treasure you, for in this delight, of my regard for the things I have lost, I can see you. See you, in my future:

Whoever you are.

Redeem with me this note, on unwritten scales, played as Plato would have it, a note to describe the times, and the times's needs and habits and homes and ways ... and means ... the note is the means, for our decision to return:

◻

Awake.

◻

Orbiting another star. Sandra is weeping and I soothe her. The boy is asleep. I have a scar on my cheek.

She looks at me like she doesn't know me.

"My name is Dee," I tell her. But she shakes her head. Still, I stroke her hair and her trembling eases. We are approaching the blue sun.

Gol's voice begins to play on the recorder, raspy and cold:

"Welcome to Origin, Dee. Their first Temple. Now you must pull it down. The device is strapped to the hull. How you set it off is your choice. By kamikaze bomb if you like. Or bring it there and set it off manually. But the bomb will largely work on its own. You've brought it here, and we thank you. Now finish what you started."

He starts to say something else but I shut it off. I

can't stand to hear any more of his voice. The boy is waking up.

"Dad," he says. "I had a bad dream."

"It's over now. We're here."

69

The Temple

Like a castle, a temple is a place cut off, quite literally, from the world. A Black Hole into time, that holds its own ruins about it—many centuries' worth.

I have more sympathy for the Hierodules now. In some ways I am one of them. Another archivist. Is it not strange that men kill over stories?

So have I.

Once in orbit I launched quickly, alone, and entered the atmosphere in my pod, burning up. I landed in an estuary and swam through the muck to the marshy ground. The stones were nearby, and they shuddered over me.

I know the time is coming when I will be unable to go on any more adventures. Perhaps that is why I was so desperate for this one.

I strap the device to the stones and I see a face in the water—a Hierodules, a woman. Over me in the sky I see the shadow of the stones.

It must be my ancestors telling me: come home,

come home to us, we are your home. I don't deny it but it isn't right that they should know me, so far away, and so close.

The Hierodule stands behind me. He/she slips around my back. His cool body presses against mine. And the stones are filled with electricity.

He whispered a word into my ear. The word was "friend."

I felt at the center of so much—so much. We do not have words for these things. Though part of me is loathe to do it, there is another part of me that knows I must. Forgive me, again. There is so much I don't know.

I went to him and we made love.

And then we ran into the sand.

Under these stars I made a covenant, with him, never to leave. Though I have.

So many broken promises in my life.

Broken fatherhoods and marriages. Broken loves. Broken temples. Broken minds.

I used to fear I was insane but that is no longer my fear. What I fear now is that I will never understand anything, and I want to. Even though some say understanding is the enemy. But that is a Christian position, and they tend to value ignorance above all things.

If I am to be honest of what I experienced at the temple, I must part with the narrative form I have used until now.

This pains me, but it is all right. The pain of poetry expresses the pain of that place, and the pain I have carried with me from it.

But it is the stones who must answer. I will answer for the stones!

They would have their answers and I will give them their answers!

I will give them all of my answers!

This must be why we worshipped mountains, and still do. The stone itself carries this wisdom within it. It remembers things we do not and I can show it to you.

Hear me!

I am Magician!

My name is John Dee!

I have brought many thousands of years with me, in my body!

I cry to you:

It is all only one Earth! Wherever we have gone.

Numberless as the tides and seasons are my oaths. And I barter with you to build me a rock to hide behind, so that I might know thee, as a sparrow knows a boy, shadowing his feet, over the grass, and fluttering about over his head, as I have watched my boy, in these years since my departure.

These stones hear me. They are part of me. Part of the planet. What can I do with stones? It is what they do with me.

They show me the world.

This is the world:

It is Margaret. A woman I knew in England. Long before I met you.

It is the world behind the world. In dreams.

It is my cloak.

My staff.

It is my honor guard about me, in my raiment, and with stones in my hands. Good for drowning, should I need it, and good for passing around too, to discuss. These stones are me. I am these stones. I carry them with me wherever I go.

Black lines scatter over the great arch.

I am going in.

To town.

Come with me to town, and I will show you something different, from your lover, or your friend, I will show you the world within you. Come with stone, under the sky, and I will show you how to fly within.

Fly within, count me, I am a number, count me your number, in your pokcet. And I fly with thee, in my magic pocket, I am yours, a stone. Flying.

Fly me, a stone. In your pocket. In your pocket, over the land. And the sky. I am a stone. I am your stone. Dee!

(But I have been others)

Carry me a stone through the edge of the rock, to the electric battleground.

These edges are what I need now, like the game of Go.

Electric me Go. Pause me pace me thrill me advance me build me screw me shape me and stand me up.

Stand me up. I am a basement. I am a basement tunnel. I am a basement tunnel in your heart.

I am a basement tunnel in your heart! I will live! I

will live, as long as you do!

Build me up. Raise me over the marshland, bog dweller!

Raise me over the marsh and I go. I can take you with me, if you want to go.

Is it so bad to leave?

Dance with me.

Hey, will you stand to see the stars with me. Don't be miffed if we don't have milk today, or swords, or mouths, or hands, or evil things to do, if we are only this, numberless as the rain, charter numbers, characters in a world, marks.

Mark, mark me, fast and slow, over the pavement. Tell me where I need to go, I am a mark over the pavement. I am a cut in the grass.

(A Temple is a cut in the grass).

I am a pavement cut in the grass and you must tell me where to go.

You must lead me too. Try me for you and tell me: what direction is it?

Lean in and see: what direction is it leaning?

Who is it going to?

What god speaks slow over the mountains. What

woman whispers in your ear?

Woman, come here, and whisper to me too.

"I've been looking for you Dee."

"Ha ha ha!"

"Always joking Dee."

We are dancing. Still she is whispering into my ear, of love.

I am not capable of love. I am, but it is imperfect love. Ruined and dark. It is musical love. Terrible love. It is death!

"Shhhhh."

I am Dee. I am going now, never to return!

"Don't go, Dee."

I will go, never to return!

"If that's what you want."

These stones, what are they?

"They've been here forever. We've been here for-ever."

And why? Why is it?

"We don't know Dee."

But I want to know! Tell me!

"Shh, Dee, shhh."

Tell me!

"All right, Dee. Long ago there was a man came here, with a staff made out of ash., 'Do you have berries?' he asked. I didn't but I offered him my body and he took me under the oak, where I died. I died for him. Then my name oak. I am Oak, Dee. I stand by water. Looking for men, to come to me."

I am stone, aren't I? I had forgot!

"Yes, Dee. You are stones!"

I kissed them, the stones.

The Hierodule was gone.

What is this Earth, that it says so many things to us? Changing us into dangerous things. Magic things. It just happened.

Gol's bomb is blinking.

I must deactivate it. No one should harm these stones.

I call my ship, phone pressed against my face.

"Dee."

"Gol. Tell me how to deactivate the bomb."

"You don't get to deactivate it."

"We mustn't destroy these stones!"

"This world is lost. That is as it should be."

"No!"

I took the bomb and ran into the marsh.

What I became then I still do not understand. I was in multiple places at once. Power flowed through me, like a whole Earth moving. I was awake but I was far away, standing in the marsh.

My phone was on the ground, in the mud. It squawked at me:

"Dee! Dee!"

A hole was burnt in my chest. I activated the launch pod and was propelled into orbit, sealed in its cocoon.

Much of this document I wrote in that pod, waiting to be rescued.

70

Returning

People say science and religion are at war. Like the land and the sea. War is not the right word. They are related, science and religion. A shifting family of realities.

In some ways saving the First Temple of the Hierodules was the best thing I've ever done. The feeling of that place remains with me to this day, like a thin and beautiful scar in the mind.

I aged a great deal on the return trip home, to Earth.

I am like an electron to the nucleus that is Los Angeles. One day I will be a photon, and leave it forever . . .

Though not today.

▫

Semira is not well. She is in the hospital, wanting morphine.

I press the button for the nurse.

"She's not good," the nurse says to me in the hall, after Semira has gone to sleep. "You should think about letting her go."

"I know."

All the friends I have lost. With more still to lose.

Sandra is in Silver Lake, with our son.

"You want to come in?" she says.

"Thank you."

"Do you want tea?"

I watch her pour the water into the kettle. All these years and she is still beautiful. Like Los Angeles is beautiful.

"You're made of magic," I tell her.

She puts her hands on her hips and looks out at the lake. They keep a fence around it so no one will swim in it.

"I think we should dismantle that fence," I tell her.

"You'll be arrested. I won't bail you out."

"No?"

"No, I won't."

"How's Johnny doing in school?"

"He's doing well."

"How are you doing?"

"When are you going?" she asks.

"Tomorrow."

71

New Orleans

I am Jacob Cerrig. In, as they say, a former life.

I knock on the door. The man that answers is a Hierodule. I can see it in his eyes.

"Hello," I say. "Francis?"

"Come in," he says.

I follow him into his living room.

"Do you know Henry Cerrig?"

"We lived together seven years. A common law marriage, ha ha!"

Chimes sound outside the window. The windows are stained glass. Francis goes to a book shelf, takes out a volume and brings it over to me.

"This here was our achievement," he says, opening the album.

It's a temple; I can see that. A younger Francis and another man stand outside a small building framed by trees. It looks like a hippy pagoda.

"We built something inside it," Francis says. "Henry worked hard. Harder than many men. But it was something he carried inside him. Some separateness. It's what I loved about him."

"How did you meet him?"

The stained glass is growing brighter.

"We met at a church group. You know what I am, John. I needed someone like your father. To build what we needed. It was good that I loved him. I still do, I think."

"Build the mandala, you mean."

"Yes."

"Where is he now?"

"What you are now, John, it's not healthy. But you know, probably as well as I do, why you had to become the way you are now."

"I don't."

"Because you were available, John. A lot of human minds, they resist the reality of our transmission. Not your father. Not you."

"Tell me where he is."

The light from the stained glass turns, like a key, or a stage effect, when time is passing in a play. Blue stars rotate over yellow and green, painting a circle on the far wall. Francis goes to the circle and presses his hands against the wall. The room grows dimmer.

Francis presses against the wall, and the sunlight is almost gone. The lamp by his face burns brighter, hot white light. Then it dims too, and we're sitting in the dark.

Stars pass overhead.

I feel the couch press against my back.

Another room is appearing now. Wooden drawers line the walls, some of them splintered.

"Come, this way."

I stand and follow him, through the grove of trees, covered in deep green vines and bark of all colors. I squint from the deluge of light. The only sound is wind, and the leaves under my feet.

"I haven't been here in a long time," Francis says.

A room in all white—or a sort of room, white tile and white furniture but no walls, celing or doors— nestles in the explosion of greenery. A man is crouched on one of the couches.

He looks up at me. He smiles a little.

We look at one another for a long time.

Finally, I go to sit near him on one of the couches.

I'm crying.

"Where have you been?" I say.

"I've been away a long time," he says.

He doesn't say anything. His hands are dark brown.

"I don't remember anything," I say.

"A lot of dogs in this fight. If you had remembered everything, John, you wouldn't have been able to do all the things you've done."

"Tell me what you made me forget."

"You were a pretty normal kid. Good in school. You've met Seventeen. You know they want control of this whole region of space. To monitor the minds of everyone on Earth."

"I don't know that. But go on."

"They do, John. The sum of gray matter on Earth— it's at a threshold. We're getting big, John. And if we're going to survive, we need even bigger friends."

"Tell me why you made me forget!"

I stood up. The light shifted through the trees.

"What kind of universe do you want, John? That's the question I had to answer for myself. Do you want a universe where everyone goes mad? Where everyone sees aliens all the time, and black holes, and dimensional gates, and all the rest of it?"

"Yes."

My father laughed, a tired laugh.

"I thought that way for a while. But I saw what it did to people, John. Is that what you want, John?"

"It's because they're being lied to, Harry. That's the only reason."

"The reason we made you forget is so that you would be our agent, John. So that you would make friends in Los Angeles, and find out who was working for whom. I'm sorry!"

"You're coming back with me. Seventeen is coming. They'll be here soon. You're right that I'm good at it, Dad. Will you help me?"

"No."

He looked away, out into the trees.

"I don't care. You're coming with me."

"The Church wants me dead."

"I don't care."

"You don't care if I'm murdered?"

"No. But you won't be. Come on."

I put out my hand to help him from the couch and he took it. His grip was strong.

"There's one thing, John. I never turned you into a

killer. You did that yourself."

We walked out of that place in silence. Francis took my Dad's hand, and he let him.

We didn't speak much on the plane back to Los Angeles.

Part 6:

In Orbit, and After

72

I am in orbit. Below, I can see North America. Panama does not appear to join the two Americas any longer.

I have been remembering:

□

I am on a plane, heading west. With my father.

WHICH DO YOU PREFER, DEE?

Who is that?

ELIZABETH

You're not Elizabeth.

I AM. THOUGH THAT IS NOT MY NAME. WE DON'T HAVE MUCH TIME. DECIDE FOR US. WHICH WILL IT BE: MORE TRUTH, OR LESS?

What?

YOU MUST DECIDE. I CAN MAKE YOU MORE INSANE, WHICH YOU WILL HAVE TO BECOME IN ORDER TO UNCOVER MORE OF THE ANSWERS YOU HAVE BEEN SEEKING. I CAN KEEP YOU AS INSANE AND AS SANE AS

YOU ARE NOW, IN WHICH CASE YOU WILL BE UNLIKELY TO UNCOVER ANYTHING MORE THAN YOU HAVE ALREADY. OR I CAN MAKE YOU MORE SANE. YOU WILL BE HAPPY, DEE. YOU WILL FORGET MANY THINGS. Make me more insane, then. I have to find out. What this is about.

YOUR WISH, AS THE GENIE SAID, IS MY COMMAND

◻

It is one thing to say that we are only a sort of thing in the Red King's Dream, and another to put these claims about reality into practice.

Magic is how I have done so. Magic is a form of asking the question: what world do I want to see?

What flora and fauna would I have populate this infinite beach? And what song the Piper play?

Alone above our blue dot, I rehearsed what I thought I knew.

◻

What would be appropriate?

What would mean something to me?

What would be worthwhile?

How can I get there.

What will I know.

Who will I meet, on the way.

What will I be able to endure?

What will it do to me.

Should I choose the easy one, or the hard one?

And do I really have a choice?

If I begin to understand, what then?

What can I remember. Whether the memories are real or not at this point is irrelevant. I need them.

I remember Sandra's face, and her dark eyes. I remember her raging over the sky. Over that terrible red shape larger than the Earth.

I remember Albert. I remember my son.

I remember Los Angeles.

I remember that poor boy in the alley.

I remember dreams.

I am partly dreaming now but I am awake.

Come with me, though I be a dream, and I will show you something different from this world, through doors that were not here before.

Open with me:

THIS IS SEVENTEEN. WE ARE LOCKED ON TO YOUR VESSEL

I am descending.

PLEASE IDENTIFY YOURSELF.

My name is John. John Dee.

73

The Earth

Seventeen has installed a tracking device in my neck. Of course they do not believe my story. Why would they? They assume I am a spy for the Hierodules.

These cities—as I saw on the flight my minder scheduled for me as a "new guest"—are shaped like executive washrooms. The factories are polished and arranged like the sinks, porceliain grey, around geometric art-shapes that also absorb some of the chemical waste of the manufacturing. The residential and commericial buildings appear as brightly colored bathroom stalls, squat rectangles arrayed around the trees.

"We're pushing ahead," my minder said. I didn't ask what he meant.

They have installed me in a public escritoire, perhaps to punish me for telling them a truth they did not believe, that I have been writing my memoirs. Now I live in a glass room set up in the public square.

A strange and public prison.

I give the pages to my minder. He lets me keep copies. They do not seem to mind what I write. I asked what year it was and they told me: "years do not exist." Even as Emperor Chin forbade the use of the past to criticize the present.

Are you there, Albert?

What have I done.

❑

I have considered a number of ways I might end my life. They do not lock the rooftops of their buildings here. But they can override anyone's body as you might override a car on a road: just press the button. Will they do it to me too?

I am writing. The last thing I have left.

❑

Whatever Seventeen's motives were in the time period I've left, in this time they care only for controlling the dimension gates. Scientific interest is still expressed publicly but I have not been able to find any scientists. I do not believe they exist any longer. Whatever innovation that occurs must happen in spite of the culture here.

Still, the story is the same, with Seventeen or without it. I am tied in a knot. All my decisions are at war with one another. Now I must pay the price, like Faust.

The devil lives inside, like old religious relics for a religion long dead, its priests' names faded from the walls, its gods' faces repurposed into new stories, cut from their old pedastals and installed in new temples.

In my time there were young people who imagined they were aliens. It is fortunate others did not believe them. Why, then, did people believe me?

You could stay here forever, Dee. Until you die, whenever that is. However that is. Seventeen has hinted that I am to be sent into the future. But I think they know I would manage to kill myself before I would allow that to happen, so they keep me here, and I write. The people look through the glass at the strange bear imprisoned there, hunched over his notebook, writing words in a language none of them can read. Sometimes I wave at them. Sometimes I scream. Sometimes I strip naked, and masturbate in front of them. I am the monkey in the cage.

Look at me. I am a monkey. This is my home. I live in this tree. This is my shit. This is my mouth. These are my eyes. Watch my hand move over the paper, making words you can't see. Hear my screech. My screech is this:

EEEEEEK

EEEEEEEEEEK

EEEEEEEEEEEEEEK

My family needs me.

Just decide, Dee. What will you have? You must pay for what you have done! You must accept the challenge and live too with the burden of the knowledge that you will not be punished for everything. No one has time to punish you for everyjthing, Dee.

Except the Castle.

And inside that Castle is a tower.

But remember, Dee, why you're going back: to surrrender. You will defeat no one but yourself. And it is your goal to defeat much of yourself. Weaken yourself. Unburden yourself. Shed these horrors and forget, and return, to Los Angeles, and your family. Are you decided?

(yes)

Then go.

I pick up the telephone. I tell Seventeen I have agreed to the time travel mission. They are very happy. But I know where the teleporter will take me:

74

The Castle, redux

In the dark corridor. I can smell the dust. And somewhere near, a hearth. Then I see him: Jimmy is here! My crash-landed alien friend, crouching in the corridor like an assassin. I am there too, lit by the fluorescents.

"Jimmy!" I whisper. He turns to look at me, through his black visor. I see he recognizes me but he says nothing. He turns back to the door.

A Hierodule opens it, in black robes that swirl fire from the hem, behind him a train of attendants, a school of ink fish. Jimmy turns his head away and shields his eeys, and I do as he does. When I open them I see Jimmy slip through the door and close it quietly behind him. I rush to it and tap on it.

"Jimmy!" I whisper. I press my ear to the oak. "Jimmy!"

I hear him then. "Wait," he whispers through the door.

I hear a sound on the other side of the door. The

door opens then. Another Hierodules stands there, ink flowing all around him. Some of it sticks to my skin.

"Come in, man," he says.

The Hierodule compels me to sit at the desk. But it also feels like the right thing to do. The screen lights up and its colors wash over my face. The Hierodule stands by my shoulder.

"We begin with the water," the priest says. "You know water?"

"Yes," I say.

"We shall reacquaint you with it."

The metal arm descends and catches me like a trout in a net, raising me up through the ceiling, where the priests' assistants stand and grasp me, and press my head into the water basin.

Inside the Castle there are many things. Even as within our soul are treasures uncounted, perhaps uncountable. Is my intention—no, I remember my intention. Only to go through. Whatever loss I incur on the path is exactly what I desire.

I scream as they take my head out of the basin. Then they put it back in.

◻

I am wearing white. A novice. I am a magician. I serve Los Angeles! I serve my family. Wherever they are now.

I follow my brother novice down the corridor, to the prayer room.

Our gods light around us, black circles.

We bow.

I bow.

We bow.

The gods circle round us. Inside their black ink I can see the Hierodules' eyes.

Slowly they become human again and then assemble in the center of the large room. They lead us in our exercises. There is no hunger. There is no exhaustion. There is no thought. Only my body.

My body is a tool. I am a tool of God.

◻

I am asleep in my cell. The Hierodule comes to me, the one who met me at the door. We make love in my bed.

He whispers to me, after we are finished: "I have a secret for you. On the second level, behind the altar, you will find a gate. Go through it. It may be I was wrong about you. I want to know. Go through it. If you survive, remember me. If you do not, I will remember you."

I kiss him. Though I want to slit his throat.

◻

The next morning I prepare breakfast for the brothers, then sneak upstairs to the altar. I push it rudely aside. Behind it is a small speaker-box.

"Password," it says, in its tinny voice.

"I don't have a password. The brother told me to come this way."

"What is your name?" it asks.

"I have no name. I wish only to serve."

"You're lying. What was your name before you came here?"

"John was my name. But now I am only a servant."

"You want to come through the fields?"

"Yes."

"If I let you, you must do something for me," the box squeaks.

"Yes."

"I want some of your blood."

I cut my finger with my knife and let the blood drip into the box.

"Oh!" the box says. "Can I have a little more?"

"Open the gate," I say.

"I need you," the box says, and the gate opens on yellow light.

I step through.

□

Into the field.

There is a horse here. I stroke its skin. The horse watches me carefully.

"Will you let me ride you?" I ask the horse.

I walk with it a ways through the grass.

I am going East the horse says within my head.

"May I come with you?"

I am riding East.

"What is East?"

There are other horses there.

"Let me help you."

Are you a horse?

"I am a man."

You must be a horse.

We walk on, my hand on the horse's side.

This grass is good.

"Let me ride you," I say.

You can't enter the sanctuary.

"Then take me to the edge of it. I must get through the fields."

Let us say I believe you are a horse. Then I will let you ride.

"I agree."

But if you are a horse, you must fly. Will you fly?

"I don't know. Will I?"

Ah, you are not a horse. If you are not a horse, I can not let you ride.

"Do you fly?"

I do, but not in the air. I fly in the spirit world.

"I fly there too."

Then ride me.

◻

We ride East.

There is no sun here, nor darkness. Only bright yellow light, over the fields.

If I am a man, I will protect you. If I am not a man, I will protect you.

If I am a man, I will remember you. If I am not a man, I will remember you too.

I am flying. Inside the spirit world.

I wish to forget everything that happened.

Make me Knight Parsifal. Parsifal inside his forgetfulness. Will you? Will you do that for me?

Let me forget everything.

Shhhhhh the horse says. We are riding.

◻

We come to a lake and I swim. So does the horse.

We are dreaming beneath the dark sky, without moon. There is a star overhead. It is whispering to me. I will not listen to it.

I have no name. The horse has a name. Its name

is: Horse.

The horse laughs a little at that.

I will forget everything! Everything will be taken from me!

□

Inside the Castle is dreams. Did you know the Anglo-Saxons had the same word "dream"? But for them that word meant "music." For Plato, music was the foundation of all education. And within the Castle, that foundation is dreams. Perhaps they are indistinguishable? Or, those things which converge in higher realities—dreams and music—are made of the same components, like quarks.

To navigate dreams is to navigate the soul. And some reach another shore.

□

If I forget. If I let go. It will be no different from going into the future, and letting the past slide over me. As in a dream that one wakes up from slowly, remembering the feeling long after the details are gone. So what if I can't understand anything? This is no great terror.

The horse is wide, and alive. I have coiled the hose within. I am an electric spark. Wooo woooooooooooooooooooooooooooooooooo

Tell me I have forgotten already. Tell me I am forgiven

You are neither.

But that's what I want, Horse.

Let me tell you something. You're getting better. Don't forget. Or what worth would you be?

Faster, horse.

We'll get there in our own time. Tell me, why are you in such a hurry to forget?

I'm afraid, horse. If I can forget, then perhaps I can become who I was before.

That is impossible.

But people do forget, Horse.

Yes. Who do you want to become then?

I only want to be a servant, horse.

But the reason you came to me is because you don't want to be a servant. If you had wanted that, you would have stayed in the novices' dormitory.

You know about that?

We are approaching the sanctuary. When I give the word, close your eyes.

Light is spreading over the strange sky. The field is infinite. But I can see a building in the distance, like a barn made out of stone.

Now close them.

I do. The wind is loud. I grip the horse's neck. We're flying . . .

Then I am on my feet. The horse is running to the barn, in the distance. I am alone.

Ask for permission to enter. It is possible my family will permit it.

"Hello?"

The wind is howling. Clouds rush over the sky.

"Hello, is anybody there?"

"Hello?"

Ask.

"Can I come inside?"

There is a grey horse watching me, from the eaves of the barn.

"May I please enter your sanctuary?"

The grey horse stands still.

"I'm trying to get back to my family."

Why did you leave them then.

"I don't remember."

Come inside then, and sleep. But you must leave in the morning. And you may not enter the building.

I cross the invisible line and walk towards the barn. The clouds are accelerating, along with the wind.

I clear a patch of earth and start a small fire to warm myself.

This prairie reminds me of so many things. The warmth of the fire is real enough.

My memory is not improving. But that is what I wanted. My instincts are all that keep me going. Are they good enough?

Go to sleep. We will watch over you.

I close my eyes, and listen to the sounds of horses inside.

◻

There is no sun but morning has come. Horse nudges me with his nose.

Come. Where do you want to go?

"To the mountains."

Then that is where we will go.

□

"Are there many of you horses here?"

Many.

"How long have you lived here?"

Eternity.

"That's a long time."

Not so long. It's over quick.

"What is your name?"

My name is Fire Rush Through Wind and Rain Run South By the Reeds After She Came To Help Him.

"That is a beautiful name."

What is your name?

"I don't remember."

You remember. Tell me.

"I was John Dee. But I'm not him anymore. I don't know who I am."

That's all right. You are a horse. And you are flying.

If you like, I can give you a name.

"Yes, give me a name."

You are The Man Who Spoke To Me In The River When I Was A Boy And I Shouted At You And You Threatened Me With A Sword And I Spoke To You At Great Length About My Family And We Ate Together In The Forest After Night Had Come.

"All right. Can I have a nickname?"

Ha ha. No.

◻

I will fight your children with words. I will carry them on mountains. I will throw them into the sky. I will breathe with them in water. I will fly with them in air. I will dance.

I will dance.

Remember me when I am gone.

We ride through the river and move into the foothills. We are coming to the tower of the magician.

Help me. I will escape the Castle. But when I do, you must remember for me who I am. Because I will not remember. Somewhere inside of me will be the information. It may be in you too. I don't know. Wait for me. I'm coming!

□

There are people here, standing in the grass at the base of the tower.

I wish you well.

"Goodbye."

I watch Horse run back West. The people are coming for me and they lift me up, onto their shoulders, carrying me into the tower.

My name Dee was a river. I am coming to a river again, but not of water.

Like the jetstream.

Cartesian coordinates.

Position and velocity, and a curve:

Up the stairs, held by their hands. They are smiling.

"Let me walk," I say.

"We mustn't. You'll be working soon enough."

Up the stairs.

I feel the eyes on me, and not just these people.

Your purpose is to escape, Dee. You mustn't forget.

"We will let you escape," one of the women gripping me says. "But first you must work for us."

Labor is related to an older word for "totter," as under a burden.

This weight, of you. And my weight, for you. I am placed in the chair.

"Strap him in."

I am in the chair.

"Dee, you're going higher up."

"All right," I say.

"Don't be afraid. We're here for you."

"What do I do when I get there?"

"Fight for us."

They attach the helmet, and the mouth guard.

They lower the curtain, so I can not see out over the balcony of the tower.

"Are you ready?"

"Yes."

"Count backwards from ten."

"Ten, nine, eight …"

75

Shelter

I am under the sky. But not far under it.

I am a mendicant. A courtier.

I am Jacob Cerrig. I take by the heel.

A higher floor of the Castle.

There is a boy in the courtyard.

"Young man, I am newly arrived. Tell me, who rules here?"

"Why, we do, sire."

"You have a democratic government?"

"Perhaps it's the Secretary you're wanting? She usually greets new arrivals. Where are you from?"

"Far away. Earth."

"Hmm. Yes, see her."

I follow the boy's directions and go into a public building. The light is strange—purple and red, from sconces on the walls. A womans sits behind a desk with various colored pamphlets scattered over it.

"Yes?" she says.

"Does this keep have a ruling constabulary?"

"Ha ha! No. We have no need of additional defense. Who are you?"

"My name is Jacob. Cerrig. I'm from Earth."

"Hmm. Is that a Field? An Ordinated Locale?"

"It's a planet."

"A planet. Hmm. In what galaxy?"

"The Milky Way."

"Never heard of it. Well, here, take these pamphlets, they should get you settled. Dinner's at eight, in the hall, unless you fancy hunting, which you can do, but the season is almost over. Do you have a weapon?"

"Only my staff."

"You may keep that. Welcome to Shelter. You're really from a planet?"

"Yes."

"It's strange … you remind me of someone. No matter. See you for dinner!"

I sat outside under the trees and browsed the pamphlets.

"So You've Decided to Leave Reality Behind," is the title of one of them. Another is "Cosmic Ideas Clearly Explained." They're very handsomely made, with glossy photographs of good looking people. A third is entitled "Scrubbing the Well is a Good Meditation." I open this one.

The opening paragraph states:

"Toothbrushes work well on the stones. Be sure to check your work with others. Every dream counts. We can't eat without it."

The photographs depict a working team furiously scrubbing a stone well with toothbrushes. Below it, a diagram with arrows points to little bubble universes, connected to the well.

"Hello," says a young woman. "The Secretary tells me you're Jacob."

"Yes, that's me." I stand up and shake her hand. She shows me to the battlements. Her name is Evelyn, she tells me.

"Your dress is quite lovely," I tell her.

"Thank you. What were you planning on doing here?"

"I represent some of the people of Earth. My home."

"Well, I wish you luck with that. But what I meant was, what work are you planning to do with us here? You don't seem like a hunter to me."

"No, I'm not. What work do you do?"

"I pick the berries," she says, smiling. "They're quite difficult."

"Perhaps I could help with that."

"It requires a high pain threshold!"

"All right."

"Come to the grove tomorrow morning."

The hall is full of people. Mostly I don't understand what people are saying, so I just eat. They give me a mat, and I sleep by the fire. My sleep is blissfully free of dreams.

◻

In the morning I ask the way to the grove. Birds of many colors are speaking from above. Evelyn is standing under the fruit trees, watching me.

"You made it," she says. "Are you ready?"

"Yes."

"This way, my little Eve," she says, smiling. I climb the ladder at her direction. "You have to grasp hard on the fruit. Go head."

I take hold of the red fruit, like a dark pomegranate.

"Don't listen to the tree now." She slaps my hand away from the fruit. "If you take too long your hand will get stuck on there, and we'll never get you off! Do you understand?"

I nod, and try again. I grasp another fruit fiercely, and pull. I feel the tree give, like a wave, bending.

Evelyn frowns. "No. You have to concentrate. The tree wants you here. But we do not. We want you to take from the tree. You must take from it, you understand?"

"All right."

I yank it quickly and it falls into my hand, spilling dust.

"Now put it in the basket. The quicker you go the easier it is. Don't give yourself time to think."

I go to work on the tree. The fruits are little pistols, waiting to go off. I avoid looking at them until the last instant, when I yank them off their branch. Then I drop them in the basket and don't look at them. I keep my eyes focused on the distance, through the leaves, or on Evelyn, in her work smock, on her tree down the lane.

After half an hour hour I have a full basket and descend the ladder.

"Good work," she says. "But is this an honest sacrifice?"

"What do you mean?"

"You must mean it. Or it can't be done. Or we can't eat. Do you understand?"

I see now: as the brochure explained. Each fruit is a person. We're killing them.

I walk away from the grove and do not look back. I am a stupid man, I know that. Perhaps I will grow smart in time. Or perhaps what Los Angeles needed was a stupid man.

The battlements seem higher now. I go to the work detail where jobs are posted.

One reads:

"ENGINEER

Must like oil.

The Basement."

I ask my way and descend a stone staircase ten floors, through the gloom.

◻

He must like my face because he doesn't falter when I tell him I've never done any engineering. He puts me by the fire, shoveling coal. It soothes me, though it is exhausting.

What did the people of my tower expect me to do for them here? Perhaps it was this, in a way. Keeping fires lit. The shovel gives me blisters and the foreman chides me, giving me gloves. The fire's heat and glow give me a feeling of peace I haven't had for a long time.

When the workday is finished I climb the stairs and watch the sun set over the walls. The hall is mostly empty. The cook gives me a bowl and tells me that everyone is outside. I walk to the garden and see people eating the fruit.

Enceiderich, Herr Dee. Mr. Grabs by the Heel. Mr. Celtic River. Orange was a Celtic River too and look how it turned out, eh? Look how it turned out. It turned into Elizabeth.

And the beginning of the English Empire . . .

It was your idea, Dee.

These fruits were your idea.

Evelyn looks up at me with the red juice around

her lips and gestures for me to join them. I return to the basement, and the coals.

I huddle by its heat. What does my tower want? Not all of them dead; things would collapse. I am a courtier, as I introduced myself. But there is no king. No queen.

I find I have nodded off by the fire. I stand up and brush myself off, and climb the stairs again.

Evelyn's room is above the hall, with a window looking out on the gardens. I knock on her door.

"May I come in?"

She stands aside from her door and I go in.

She looks at me carefully, closing the door.

"Who are the fruit?"

"Our food, John. Many people."

"I need to know which ones."

She comes closer to me, and places her hand against my cheek.

"We don't know, John. We never will."

I grab her hand. "I want you to find out!"

"No!" she screams and the room shifts. Black smoke pours out of the walls and I throw her over my shoulder and leap out the window, into black time.

She is still screaming but she makes no sound.

I am a magician. I will find you, whoever you are. Whatever your name is, I will rip out your soul like a rag. And then I will set it afire.

76

Black Stones

If one could recover from reality, I would. As from a sickness.

Perhaps that is what I have been doing: getting well.

These stones hover in darkness, while Evelyn floats over my head.

I need to go home, but not yet. Not enough gates are sealed. And not enough others opened. I put Evelyn on one of the Stones and walk into the darkness.

Albert is there.

"I think it's working, Dad."

"Is it?"

"You're changing things."

"I have to go back. I promised."

"It's not your tower."

"Temporarily."

I ruffle his hair.

I walk past the Stones; they are carrying Evelyn up, into the black sky.

ᛚᛚ

Shelter

I walk through the hall and down to the courtyard.

"You are all cowards! Feeding off of the poor! It will destroy you eventually, but if I have my way you will be destroyed sooner!" I shout.

For my troubles I am arrested and shackled in the dungeon.

Implicated in Evelyn's disappearance.

◻

Behind the wall I hear a voice.

"Dee. You want to get out of there?"

It's Jimmy.

"Reach under the stone behind your back."

I strain my hand as far as it can go on the chain, and reach into the drain.

I feel him press a vial into my hand.

"It eats metal."

I pour it over the shackles and watch the smoke

rise. I smash them against the stones. A paving stone lifts at the center of the room then. Jimmy's head pops out, with his wild hair and huge dark glasses.

"Come on then. You should fit."

▫

Down a dank corridor cut into the rock.

"The Castle eats my people too, you know."

"Are you okay?"

"Me? Right as rain. Right as rain. Just as soon as we get out of here."

"Jimmy. I promised some people I would help them. But I don't know how. They live in a tower. My tower."

"And?"

"Will you help me destroy the Castle?"

"Don't you think I wanted to do that! I've been trying! No, I'm getting out. If you want to get out with me, then come on."

"I'll follow you to the Gates."

We swim under the portcullis and into the river.

The light is astonishingly bright.

Horse is standing there.

Shall I give your friend a lift?

"Yes."

His red body clutches Horse's large grey one, like a living cape, receding into the grass.

Part of the Castle is Los Angeles too, I know. God knows what destroying it will do to my city.

But if I wish to be redeemed, this should be my final deed, before forgetfulness comes. Before I forget what I have done I want to remember the feeling of vengeance.

What will it feel like? Will it be cold, or hot? Will it be glorious? Or disappointing? All of the above, I think. A feast after a famine. And then nausea.

I turn back and regard the Castle, or anyway, this tip of it. A little medieval dream set into the warp and woof of things, like a gland within a brain, ordering reality around its curved robes of flesh.

I remove my cape. I step forward, then back again. I look up at the sky, and move my feet.

I am dancing.

Hay hummmmm

Hay hay hummmmmm

The black shadow of Evelyn curves over the battlements then, a terrible Wight with huge black eyes. She is still female; I can feel her.

I am dancing, while black whips from her body swish past my limbs, like daggers.

I am dancing.

The thing Evelyn is screaming, as she did when I ripped her from her bedchamber, only now the sound is lower, like thunder mixed with machinery under stress.

I was born in a town in Texas.

I am a man, dancing.

Beneath these walls.

I have a love. In a city of dreams by the ocean.

I will still return to her.

What will I remember?

How much of this will make sense?

I am dancing.

The black thing Evelyn wraps tight around me like a vise, like her whole body is a cunt, sent to squeeze me to death. And I wail and twist within it, storming the winter of her thoughts, with my darker light.

I am a darker light, Evelyn. I can see past you, and

through you.

TELL ME MORE BIG BOY

You're dying.

LET ME DIE WITH YOU

Do so. So I can burn your home.

She's screaming, while I dance.

These words are mine, and no one else's. Die, Evelyn!

She makes a sound, somewhere far away.

Die!

I dance faster and carry her away.

◻

A Castle is a shelter. From what? From people. From the sky. From God.

Leave shelter and confront the world. See the world and let it see you.

We are transformed.

I'm dying.

NOT YET JOHN

Yes.

NOT YET JOHN

◻

She is dead in the grass.

I enter the portcullis and set fire to the keep.

Horse comes and takes me away, through the groves. I burn everything I see.

◻

"Where is Jimmy?"

I took him to his ship. He is a strong horse.

"Yes he is. Have you met many people out here?"

You mean, many horses?

"Yes."

Yes, many. Have you?

"Will you come to Los Angeles with me?"

I've never been there.

"All the more reason to come."

I'll consider it.

◻

I awake.

The people carry me down from the chair. They carrry me down the steps of the tower and strap me to Horse, who is waiting. My muscles have atrophied. I hold on to his mane.

"You're in several places at once," I mumble.

All horses are.

I can smell the burnt Castle in my nose. I can hear the screams of the fruit trees.

The wind smells beautiful though. As though I could live again, after I had died. Perhaps that's what this is, the afterlife. Or something like it.

That's not what it is.

"Ha ha ha, what is it then?"

Everywhere.

◻

I sleep outside the Santuary and the horses are singing within.

I dream, for the first time in a long while. I dream of Sandra, but sometimes she looks like the Princess.

I am on a boat, over dark shimmering water. With all these women's voices in my head. Like lullabies, over a neverending night.

❏

The door returning to the Hierodules' domain is burnt, just charred stumps standing crooked in the field.

We'll need another way back.

"Do you know one?"

Yes, but it's far.

"Let's go."

Wait a moment.

Horse is listening to something.

"What is it?"

The Gate you came through isn't safe. Something has taken control of it.

"Seventeen."

Perhaps. I can smell it in the air. Your tribe of horses is very wasteful.

"That's an understatement."

The way I know will be very far. Are you well enough for it?

"I can do it."

Hold on.

78

Riding

The patter of his hooves holds me in a blanket of time, warm and steady. The lilt of the sunlight grows more painful by the hours—the sun is so close!

Close your eyes.

"I'm awake, I'm awake."

Close your eyes, it'll be all right.

There is only the sound of his hooves. Into the bright night.

When I was a small horse I went to a creek and you were there. That's why I named you. You were older. And frightened. You touched my nose with your hand. I still remember you.

"How old are you?"

I am one of the seasoned ones of our herd. We count by stories, which are very long. I have told three of them.

"Like the Norse. They told long stories."

I may not live to tell a fourth.

"I hope you do."

Tell me about Los Angeles.

"They don't have many horses there."

Why not?

"It's a mechanized city. Although, with the new aliens, perhaps horses will come into style."

Is there much grass?

"Some. More asphalt than grass."

We shall have to make more grass.

"All right."

Go to sleep. It's easier for me to ride when you're silent.

79

Los Angeles, redux

I can feel something coming. Something I've been dreaming of. What is it? The energy in the air, like nothing I've ever experienced.

Also, the air stinks. People have been bringing their cars back out; I'd been getting used to a quiet city.

A friend of mine with property in Studio City has put Horse up; he seems to enjoy the weather.

My son was happy to see me. All I could do to keep from crying. Sandra was less happy, but she did give me a hug.

What is this feeling. Like waking from a dream and finding parts of it were real. Like that, but not as terrifying. More logical. As though some deep gears of reality I had always known were there have begun to turn, and things are better for it.

The Church of S. is back in the streets in their blue robes, protesting the new religious taxes. But even they seem muted.

Semira is getting better. She looks like a different

person—so much older. But better. She told me she wanted to be a nurse. We'll see if it lasts.

◻

It is a blessing that one can forget things. I haven't forgot as much as I wanted, but at least one thing I forgot turned out all right: I forgot all about Jake Smiley.

The guy was dead in the subway, run over not by a train, but by a moose.

"How did the moose get down there?" I ask the paperboy.

"You gotta read it to believe it, guy. Two bits. Two bits for an honest face like yours."

I buy the paper and read the story but it doesn't answer my question.

"Smiley's dead?" I ask him again.

"Dead as a doornail. Death comes for us all. You gonna keep that paper, or you want to donate it back to the cause?"

I hand it back to him and go into the bodega to buy a banana. On the television, one of the aliens has just been elected mayor. He raises both tentacles into the air.

"We got an alien mayor now," I tell the Korean grocer.

The grocer looks at me like I am the alien and hands me my change from his medical-gloved hand.

Outside, I see Meritzia getting into a cab. The thing is, Los Angeles has always been a small town, but it was never the kind of small town where you could bump into people: everyone's either in their apartment, or their car. But that's been changing.

I hail a robot cab, waving wildly.

"Follow that car," I tell the robo.

"Which, car, please?"

"The one right in front of you!"

"Has that auto given you permission to follow it, sir?"

"Goddamn it, I said FOLLOW THAT CAR!"

The robo gives me a careful look. "That'll be fifty bucks extra."

I slam the note into the robo's hand, and he pulls into traffic. Meritzia's headed west on Sunset.

"Can't you go any faster?" I shout at the robo.

"This cab is traveling at its maximum legal speed."

"Speed up!"

The robo grudgingly eases down on the accelerator.

"Pull up along side!"

I lean out my window and wave at Meritzia, gesturing for her to roll her window down.

She gives me an annoyed look and taps her driver on the shoulder; they shoot ahead.

"That robo knows how to drive! Don't lose her!"

"You could make me lose my license, sir."

"I'll buy you a new one! Go!"

We crest the hill west of Alameda and suddenly she's gone.

"Stop! Goddamn it!"

Then I see the cab, pulled over by a fence on the opposite side.

I empty the contents of my wallet into the robo's lap and run across the road.

Behind the fence, she's slipped around a corner. I hop up onto the chainlink.

I make an ill advised leap from the top, half breaking it with a roll but I come out of it with a twisted ankle, cursing. I speed-limp the rest of the way to the building, around the corner. It's another speakeasy, the kind of establishment no Act of God or political revolution can affect in Los Angeles. A small sign over the door reads: Junkyard.

"Who are you?" the bouncer asks.

"My name's Dee. Mind if I come in?"

"Who knows you?"

"Meritzia."

"Meritzia who?"

"I don't know her last name."

"Get lost, guy."

"Listen, I really need to talk to her."

"And now it's time for you to leave." The beefy man rolls out of his pose along the wall and takes a step towards me. He stands over me by a good foot and a half.

"You got it."

I walk-limp quick back around the corner, and then duck around the other corner to the window. Some pretty ladies are leaning half out of it, with closed eyes and sweaty faces.

"Ladies, could you give me a hand through the

window."

"Oh god, it's so hot," one of them says.

"Please, ladies."

The brunette puts down her drink and grasps my hand; she's surprisingly strong.

I tumble through the window and stand quickly.

"Do you work out?" I ask her, but she ignores me completely, already meditating.

Meritzia's disappearing down the steps in the corner of the room; I catch a flash of her dress. I hold onto the banister and move down carefully, step by step, sparing my foot.

"Meritzia!"

She's gone, off into a darker room, by the landing.

Dancing again. What is it about dancing? The universe, and people: dancing. I move in to the crowd and gyrate best I can with only one good foot, keeping an eye on her hair as she glides through the bodies.

The magic of California, and the magic of America, still transcendental even today: its earthiness is a balm to me. I shake my hair and sweat, moving slow towards the corner where Meritzia is talking to a man who looks suspiciously like Jake Smiley.

He sees me and grins, then disappears into another back room. Meritiza looks at me. There's something in her eyes, like what I saw in the boy's eyes, in that alley, in what seems like a lifetime ago. It might as well be. What is it? What does she see in me? It's fear in her eyes, and something else . . .

Then she's gone too, and the dance floor gets tighter and the music louder—I'm forced to dance with the tight packed bodies for another minute.

When the song merges into a slower one I make it to the corner. The black door in the corner is locked.

I grip it uncontrollably and shake it, leaning my good foot against the door, I tug on it. Uselessly.

At that instant the door opens. It's Semira.

"Semira?"

"John."

"What are you doing here, Semira?"

"Come downstairs."

I follow her through the door. She's wearing red, her favorite color. The feeling of déjà vu is overwhelming.

"I'm sorry I shot you," I find myself saying.

"You didn't shoot me, John."

"I'm sorry, though."

She pauses on the woodesn staircase and looks back at me. She presses her finger to her lips.

I follow her the rest of the way down the stairs, then through a dark green curtain.

There are more people in this room. It's dark. It feels like a concert only there is no music. Everyone's standing around, waiting. In the distance I can make out a stage. Then the curtain opens.

A huge man is standing there. The largest man I have ever seen.

"Who is that?" I ask Semira.

"Mary," she whispers.

His skin is dark brown. He must be at least eight feet tall, and his arms and legs are enormous to the point of being grotesque. He stands motionless.

The music starts.

"What are you doing here, Semira?"

"I'm sorry John."

The lights go up on stage. Dancers emerge from the wings. Their faces are painted black. They throw their heads back and twist their shoulders from side to side, as though they're having convulsions. Hugibert comes on stage then, and lightning effects play over the audience. He has a microphone in his hand. He holds it close to his mouth and speaks into it:

"Ee mo emmo eemo emmo enwo enmo eelie emlo noll raylinembo ainli embo rembo den meno porth-eynto …"

It doesn't make any sense to me but it electrifies the audience. The dancers on stage freeze, and then start to move very slowly towards the huge man. The audience is thrashing their boies wildly. Semira is sucked into a vibrating nexus of bodies. I back against the wall.

Then it's Meritzia on stage. Her face painted in red stripes. She shouts into her mic:

"A new world!"

My namesake's fondest dream.

I press to get out of the crowd but they're dancing ever more wildly.

"A new worrrrrrrrrrld!" she shouts again, and out of the corner of my eye I see a gas-mask-like contraption fall from the catwalk and Hugibert straps it onto the giant's face, with the help of a ladder.

"Let me out!" I shout, but the music is deafening.

Hugibert finishes attaching the gas mask and the stage lights up red.

Hugibert whispers into the mic: "Let's hear it for Mary."

The giant screams and the music stops. The dancers stand perfectly still. Some of the audience continues to thrash but most are enthralled by the sound of the giant's voice.

I grab Semira's arm and push madly through the bodies to the stairs.

"Who wants to be hooked up?" I hear Hugibert say gloatingly, like a mad circus showman.

I push her up the stairs. She's crying.

"I want to stay, John!"

"Out, now!"

I push out through the party, past the bouncer.

"Hey!" he shouts, but I ignore him, dragging Semira down the sidewalk to the street.

My phone is out of battery.

"Do you have a phone?" I ask her.

"Yes . . ."

I call a cab and we sit silently in the back, watching my city flow past.

80

Radiation

These frequencies are unbearable. I'm lying in my apartment; my head pinging with a faint, increasing headache, like a slow vise pressing against the back of my brain.

My perceptions are a curse. When will the right cells burn out so I no longer have to deal with them? Like ringing in one's ears indictates the death of certain hairs, never to return? Or will they grow back? Are such feelings ineradicable?

I feel like I'm drunk, underwater. I had taken Semira home; she promised to lie low. Now I call her and there is no answer. I call Sandra.

"John?"

"Sandra."

"What's up?"

"Could you come over?"

"I'm busy right now, John. What's the matter?"

"It's my head."

"Call 911."

"You know I can't trust them in this town."

"What do you want me to do, John?"

"Help me."

"Just take an aspirin and try to sleep. I'll be over in a couple hours."

She hung up.

◻

Why do I keep coming back to this city? One would be better off underground, or on the moon, or in some mountain range, far away …

I toss and turn on my bed, unable to fall asleep. Hours later Sandra opens my door with her key.

"You came," I say.

"I brought you some soup."

◻

She lies beside me. Biologists say humanity is a waveform … curving through time and space. And all these faster and slower signals bump into ours, cancelling, distorting, magnifying …

467

How does one tell the difference between one signal and the other? How does one tell the difference between truth and lies?

There is no telling where things might begin. Someone might arrive. A word might be spoken. A feeling could arrive in the air. A bullet could plow into your brain. I have always believed pattern recognition makes reality happen—that in this sense, no observation can ever be false, even if proved erroneous later. What we maange to piece together is the truth. And no one knows how long it will last.

Still I feel it is my duty to explain, and yet I find, more and more, that I am incapable of it. This grieves me more than I can express: so much of my life since coming to Los Angeles has been predicated on my ability to express things. My magic is based on this ability. And much of what has kept me sane in these years has been these inadequate records I have set down on paper.

Some of the things I have written I can no longer remember doing. Some of them are so vivid I can not bear to reread them myself. If anything, I find I have not spoken enough of Sandra, who has been always, at least for me, at the center this story. So let me tell just a bit about her.

She knew what she wanted—much earlier than I did. In this I find women are often the superior to men. Her writing continues to impress me, and I wish I could include some of it here, but she insisted that I should not. So I can only describe how I feel when I read it: like a bird, leaving the Earth. I have always wanted to achieve that feeling in my writing, but I feel I have never really succeeded. Her stories fly.

There is so much I never solved. In this, Los Angeles is the victor, as it is a city that insists on remaining so. New York, or Houston, even Paris, such cities can abide explanation, can solve a mystery and still move into the future. Most cities are hoarders in this way: greedy for experience, and for memories.

Los Angeles has almost no memory at all. Of course, it is a young city, and we must give it allowances. But I believe it will never grow old in the way other cities do. We can say safely of a young person that they live in the moment, that a day is like a year, and a year a century. But still nearly all young people form memories and make them into a picture of themselves. Los Angeles is not that kind of young person. It is deliberate in its destruciton of evidence. It resolutely forgets the commonest things, so as to insist they were never there at all. It is a dream city, and while such a nature has enormous charm, it is also nightmarish. One never gets an answer in Los Angeles; it is impossible.

In that sense, my own stories of Los Angeles can only accentuate this stubborn forgetfulness. It is a city better at lying than any other I have ever met. It survives by jettisoning everything, including reason. Its experiences are richer than some places, but it does not remember them.

How could such a thing have come to be? Could I find out, if I wanted to know?

I did find out about the boy. The poor boy who shot himself.

He was a new arrival.

Everyone tells themselves their own version of Los Angeles. Like a household god, kept in the mind, to nourish and nurture the imagination. We all find our own ways of reconciling ourselves with its cruelty.

The boy had become a puppet of Jake Smiley. A

woman told me this in a bar. I knew she was telling the truth. Jake had wanted the device. Perhaps he only wanted to sell it, or as a souvenir.

I had been like that boy when I came here. When I first began to tune in to the radio frequencies this region generates. One must tune a great many of them out. Listen to too many, absorb too many competing narratives, and then your own story—your self—may dissolve. I believe this is what happened to the boy. If only he had not been carrying that gun. But there are a lot of guns in America. Even now, as the Travelers and Seventeen escort us into a new future, we still hang on to our old ways. The imagined Wild West dies hard.

There is one thing I am certain of. I am becoming like Los Angeles. I am forgetting. I am jettisoning some of my old explanations, and some of my old memories (and some new ones as well). We all forget. In that empty space—so Gnostic, in many ways—we commune together.

The man named Mary has been appearing on the billboards. Sometimes I can still hear him scream. For me, LA has always had a woman's voice. But that may not be so for others. To an anthropologist, one might categorize that strange giant in that basement as only another fetish in a cult in a city famous for them.

To me, as a magician and a storyteller (however indequate), I see something else: an end of some old way of doing things, and the beginning of a new one. if we do grow comfortable inside this permament amnesia, what new feats will we perform, and endure?

□

I see Albert now, from time to time. As I used to see Foo, when he visited. Albert likes to stand on corners, like Foo did. He is a beautiful young man. He is my son. Even as Johnny is.

What I have promised myself—and Sandra— is that I will lay down my gun and leave this story behind. In fact I have sold the gun, for a good price. Though I did use it one final time. After I heard that story in the bar about the boy, I went back to the basement club.

81

Goodbyes

What I knew going in was that it would be all right. As though the city had decided I was just.

I could see already from a distance that Mary's celebration—the man-giant with the terrible voice—had spread out onto the street. Stage lights poured from the speakeasy's windows, blue and yellow through the smoke. It stretched for blocks and blocks from the site of the club, so much that I could not drive and had to take it on foot.

Revelers howled through the fog, filled with joy. Alien Travelers hovered above the house, like building-sized balloons. Someone had helpfully cut a man-sized hole in the fence and I walked through it. Any semblance of security was gone. Like Rome at festival, Los Angeles after a lock-down has a religious energy, where all things seem permitted.

I went through the door where the bouncer had stopped me and found the room empty, filled with cigarette butts and discarded plastic beer cups. An orange wig and a sun visor lay in a puddle of some lightly smoking liquid. I went around the bar to the basement door. It was open.

There was still music downstairs but it was quiet. I checked the bullets in my gun, and closed the cylinder.

It was a woman singing, about being alone. I recognized the Princess's voice. She was singing about me. About our love. Almost it made me want to abandon everything, and go to her again, and rule with her on our planet. How could I have abandoned it, and her?

She was wearing a silver dress. The crowd was pressed like Muslim worshippers against the floor, bowing motionlessly. I saw Jack in a cloud of smoke across the room. I raised my gun and fired.

◻

That feeling, that something new is coming, something to do with that giant named Mary (he has the city's name)—it has run up against my promise to Sandra, to leave this narrative behind.

My experience with the Travelers assures me I am

right to suspect my plan can be carried out as I want it to be. I am going to forget most everything, in order to prevent what would likely be my final exodus from Los Angeles—one I could never undo.

Albert has made the arrangements for me.

I am sorry for all that I did not say. I had hoped to explain my city, but now I understand this is impossible. Two books are not enough. In any case, to prevent my hand from beginning a third, I am rising into the Traveler's womb now.

Hopefully no third volume will come into existence. This will mean that I have succeeded. If you do find such a book, however, it will mean that I have failed.

Acknowledgments

A sound thank you is due to Roger Leather-wood, a fan who is also a writer. Roger read an early draft with at least as much care as I took in writing it; perhaps more.

Thank you to Alex Frankel, for being a friend. And thank you to my friends on Facebook, who are, on occasion, better than the flesh and blood kind.

About the author

Robin Wyatt Dunn writes and teaches in Los Angeles. Recently he was made a finalist for poet laureate of his city.